STAR WARS®

EPISODE V
THE EMPIRE STRIKES BACK™

VOLUME THREE

Script
ARCHIE GOODWIN

Art
AL WILLIAMSON

Art Assist
CARLOS GARZÓN

Colors
FRANK LOPEZ

Lettering
RICK VEITCH

Cover Art
AL WILLIAMSON

Cover Colors
MATTHEW HOLLINGSWORTH

DARK HORSE COMICS®

Spotlight

VISIT US AT
www.abdopublishing.com

Reinforced library bound edition published in 2010 by Spotlight, a division of the ABDO Group, 8000 West 78th Street, Edina, Minnesota 55439. Spotlight produces high-quality reinforced library bound editions for schools and libraries. Published by agreement with Dark Horse Comics, Inc., and Lucasfilm Ltd.

Printed in the United States of America, Melrose Park, Illinois.
092009
012010

 PRINTED ON RECYCLED PAPER

Library of Congress Cataloging-in-Publication Data

Goodwin, Archie.
  Episode V : the empire strikes back / based on the Screenplay
by George Lucas ; script Adaptation Archie Goodwin ; artists Al
Williamson & Carlos Garzon ; colorist James Sinclair ; letterer Rick
Veitch. -- Reinforced library bound ed.
     p. cm. -- (Star Wars)
  "Dark Horse Comics."
  ISBN 978-1-59961-701-5 (vol. 1) -- ISBN 978-1-59961-702-2 (vol. 2)
-- ISBN 978-1-59961-703-9 (vol. 3) -- ISBN 978-1-59961-704-6 (vol. 4)
  1. Graphic novels. [1. Graphic novels.] I. Lucas, George, 1944- II.
Williamson, Al, 1931- III. Garzon, Carlos. IV. Empire strikes back
(Motion Picture) V. Title. VI. Title: Episode five. VII. Title: Empire
strikes back.
  PZ7.7.G656Epi 2010
  [Fic]--dc22
                                          2009030860

All Spotlight books have reinforced library bindings and
are manufactured in the United States of America.

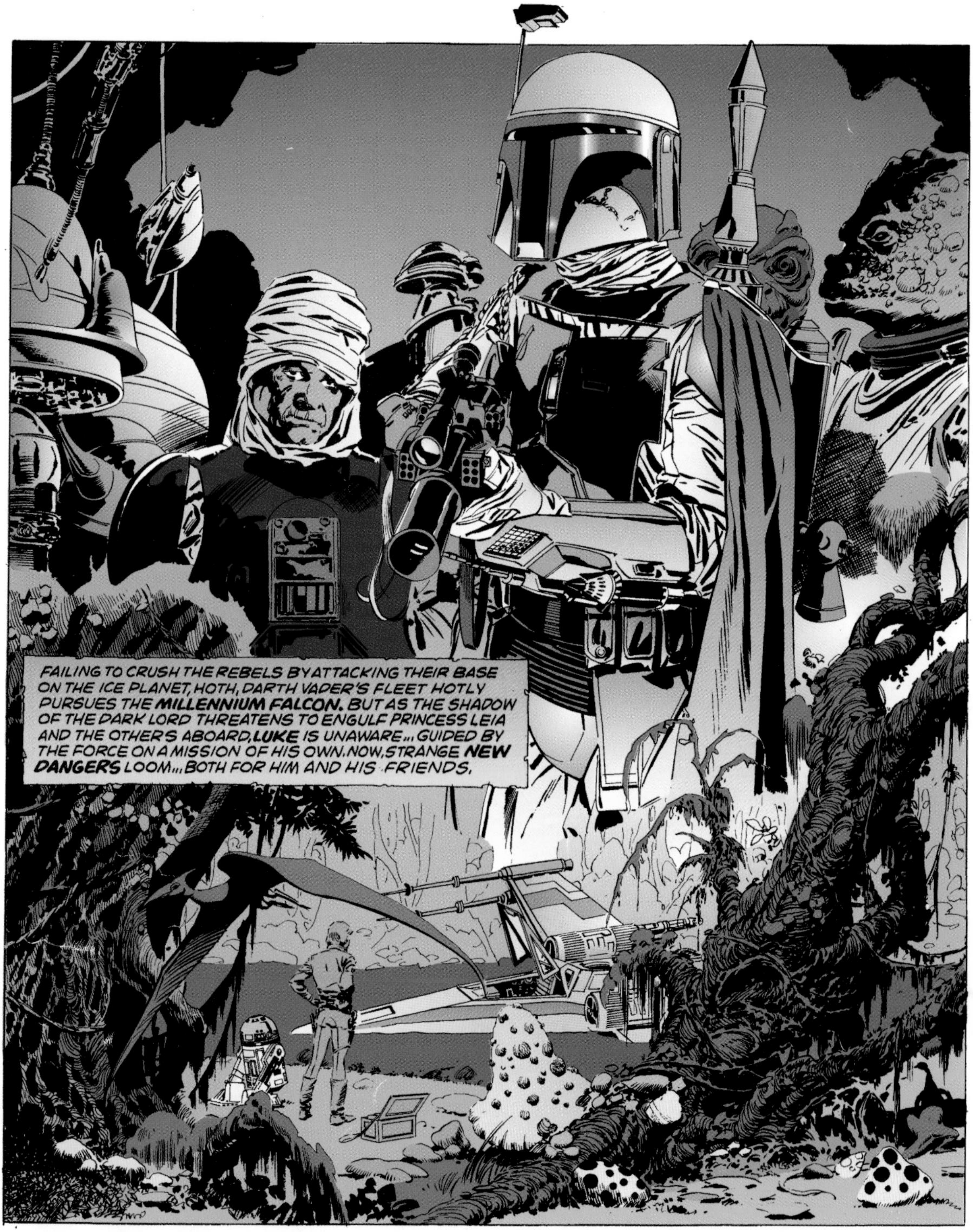
FAILING TO CRUSH THE REBELS BY ATTACKING THEIR BASE ON THE ICE PLANET, HOTH, DARTH VADER'S FLEET HOTLY PURSUES THE **MILLENNIUM FALCON.** BUT AS THE SHADOW OF THE DARK LORD THREATENS TO ENGULF PRINCESS LEIA AND THE OTHERS ABOARD, **LUKE** IS UNAWARE... GUIDED BY THE FORCE ON A MISSION OF HIS OWN. NOW, STRANGE **NEW DANGERS** LOOM... BOTH FOR HIM AND HIS FRIENDS.

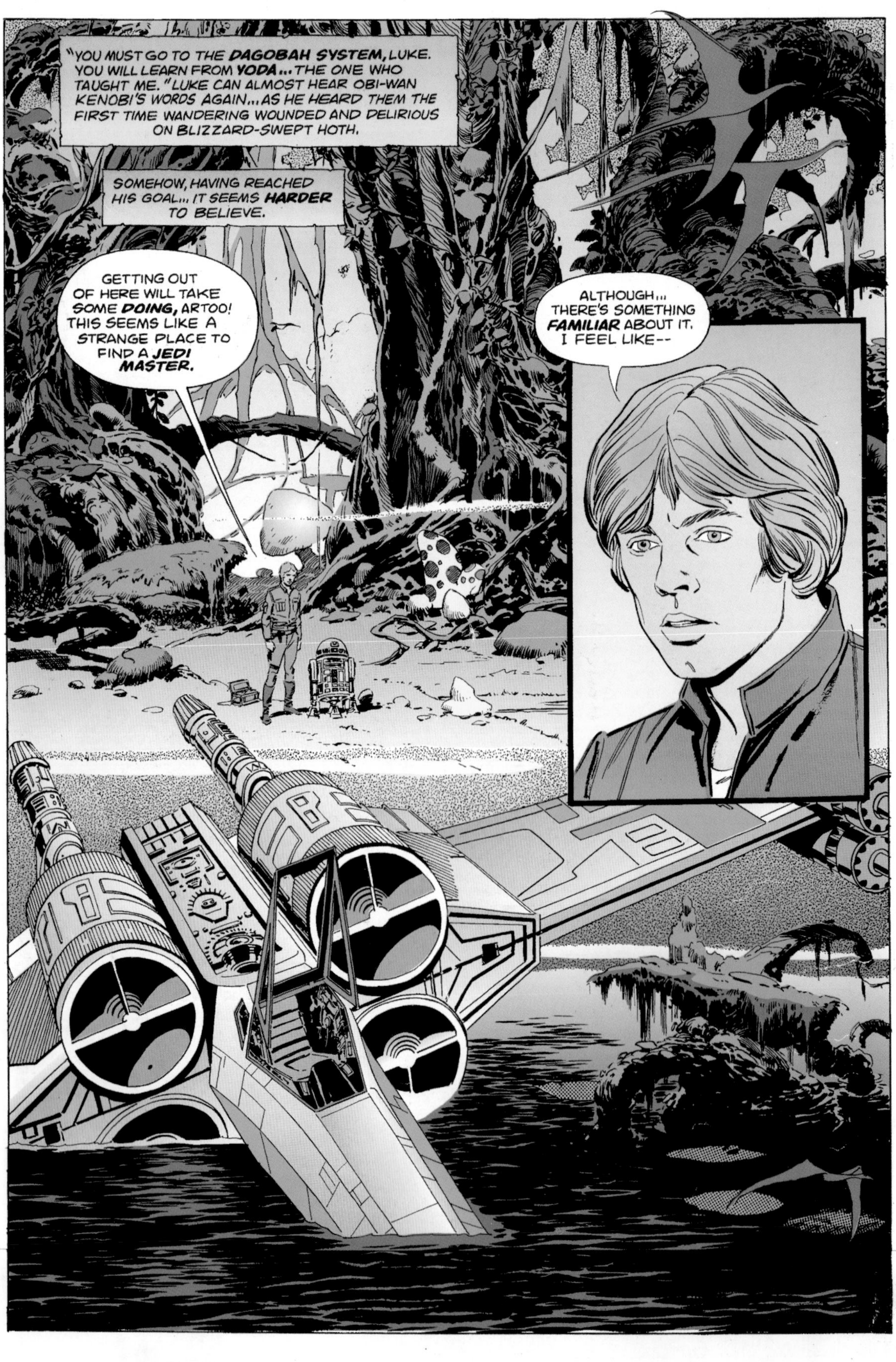
"YOU MUST GO TO THE DAGOBAH SYSTEM, LUKE. YOU WILL LEARN FROM YODA... THE ONE WHO TAUGHT ME." LUKE CAN ALMOST HEAR OBI-WAN KENOBI'S WORDS AGAIN... AS HE HEARD THEM THE FIRST TIME WANDERING WOUNDED AND DELIRIOUS ON BLIZZARD-SWEPT HOTH.
SOMEHOW, HAVING REACHED HIS GOAL... IT SEEMS HARDER TO BELIEVE.
GETTING OUT OF HERE WILL TAKE SOME DOING, ARTOO! THIS SEEMS LIKE A STRANGE PLACE TO FIND A JEDI MASTER.
ALTHOUGH... THERE'S SOMETHING FAMILIAR ABOUT IT. I FEEL LIKE--

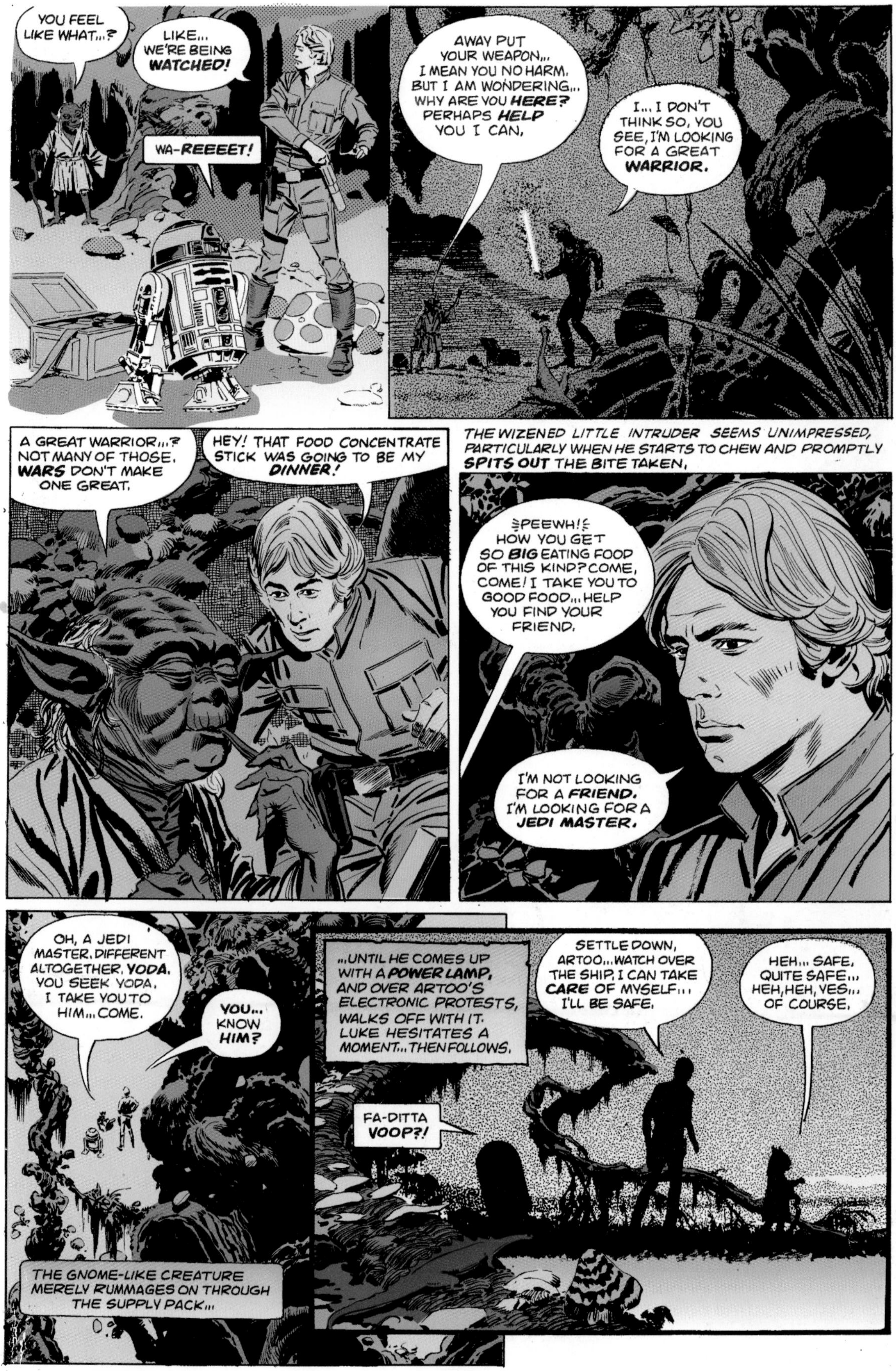
YOU FEEL LIKE WHAT...?
LIKE... WE'RE BEING WATCHED!
WA-REEEET!
AWAY PUT YOUR WEAPON... I MEAN YOU NO HARM. BUT I AM WONDERING... WHY ARE YOU HERE? PERHAPS HELP YOU I CAN.
I... I DON'T THINK SO, YOU SEE, I'M LOOKING FOR A GREAT WARRIOR.
A GREAT WARRIOR...? NOT MANY OF THOSE. WARS DON'T MAKE ONE GREAT.
HEY! THAT FOOD CONCENTRATE STICK WAS GOING TO BE MY DINNER!
THE WIZENED LITTLE INTRUDER SEEMS UNIMPRESSED, PARTICULARLY WHEN HE STARTS TO CHEW AND PROMPTLY SPITS OUT THE BITE TAKEN.
PEEWH! HOW YOU GET SO BIG EATING FOOD OF THIS KIND? COME, COME! I TAKE YOU TO GOOD FOOD... HELP YOU FIND YOUR FRIEND.
I'M NOT LOOKING FOR A FRIEND. I'M LOOKING FOR A JEDI MASTER.
OH, A JEDI MASTER. DIFFERENT ALTOGETHER. YODA. YOU SEEK YODA. I TAKE YOU TO HIM... COME.
YOU... KNOW HIM?
THE GNOME-LIKE CREATURE MERELY RUMMAGES ON THROUGH THE SUPPLY PACK...
...UNTIL HE COMES UP WITH A POWER LAMP, AND OVER ARTOO'S ELECTRONIC PROTESTS, WALKS OFF WITH IT. LUKE HESITATES A MOMENT... THEN FOLLOWS.
FA-DITTA VOOP?!
SETTLE DOWN, ARTOO... WATCH OVER THE SHIP. I CAN TAKE CARE OF MYSELF... I'LL BE SAFE.
HEH... SAFE, QUITE SAFE... HEH, HEH, YES... OF COURSE.

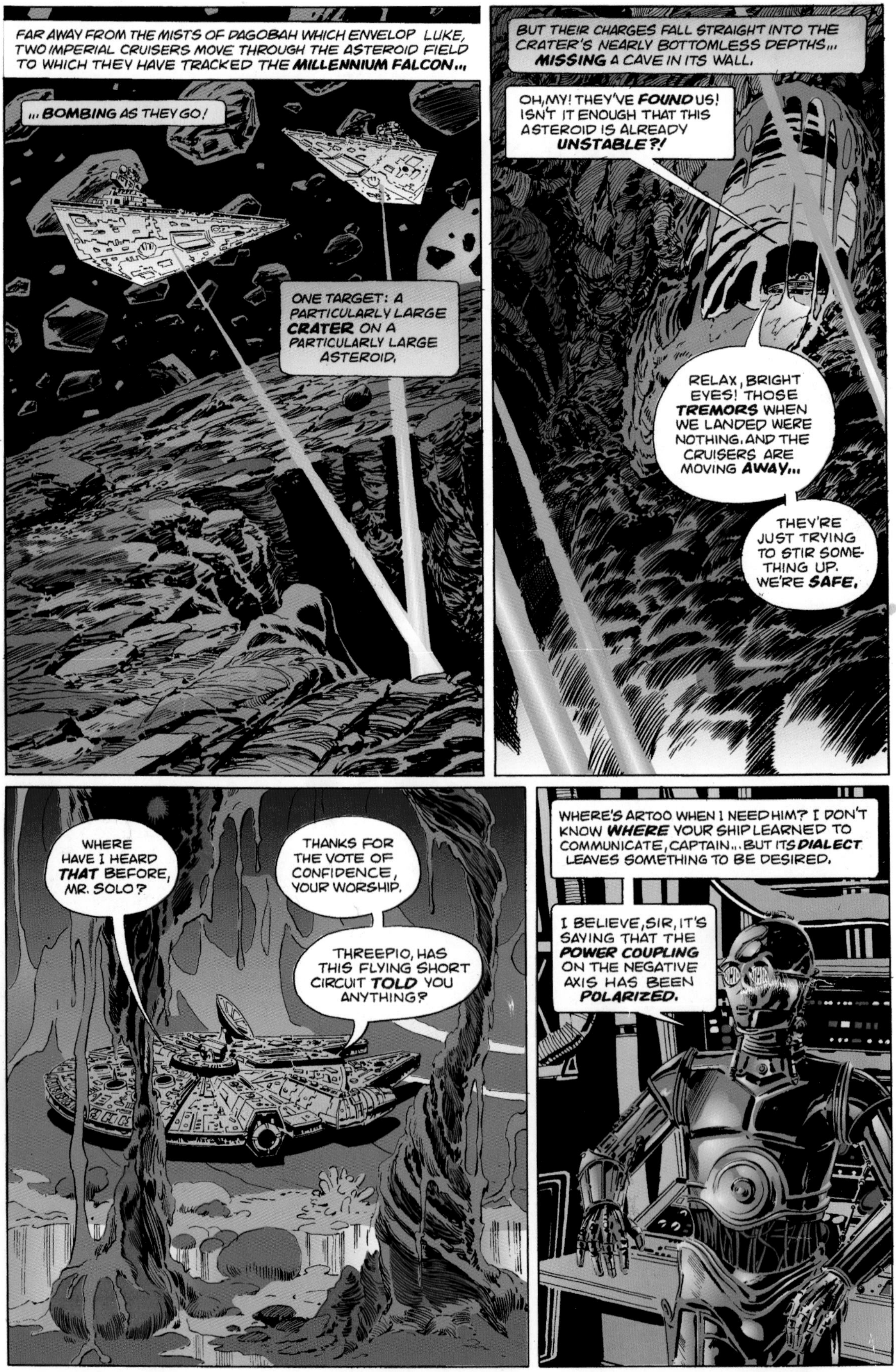
FAR AWAY FROM THE MISTS OF DAGOBAH WHICH ENVELOP LUKE, TWO IMPERIAL CRUISERS MOVE THROUGH THE ASTEROID FIELD TO WHICH THEY HAVE TRACKED THE MILLENNIUM FALCON...
...BOMBING AS THEY GO!
ONE TARGET: A PARTICULARLY LARGE CRATER ON A PARTICULARLY LARGE ASTEROID.
BUT THEIR CHARGES FALL STRAIGHT INTO THE CRATER'S NEARLY BOTTOMLESS DEPTHS... MISSING A CAVE IN ITS WALL.
OH, MY! THEY'VE FOUND US! ISN'T IT ENOUGH THAT THIS ASTEROID IS ALREADY UNSTABLE?!
RELAX, BRIGHT EYES! THOSE TREMORS WHEN WE LANDED WERE NOTHING. AND THE CRUISERS ARE MOVING AWAY...
THEY'RE JUST TRYING TO STIR SOMETHING UP. WE'RE SAFE.
WHERE HAVE I HEARD THAT BEFORE, MR. SOLO?
THANKS FOR THE VOTE OF CONFIDENCE, YOUR WORSHIP.
THREEPIO, HAS THIS FLYING SHORT CIRCUIT TOLD YOU ANYTHING?
WHERE'S ARTOO WHEN I NEED HIM? I DON'T KNOW WHERE YOUR SHIP LEARNED TO COMMUNICATE, CAPTAIN... BUT ITS DIALECT LEAVES SOMETHING TO BE DESIRED.
I BELIEVE, SIR, IT'S SAYING THAT THE POWER COUPLING ON THE NEGATIVE AXIS HAS BEEN POLARIZED.

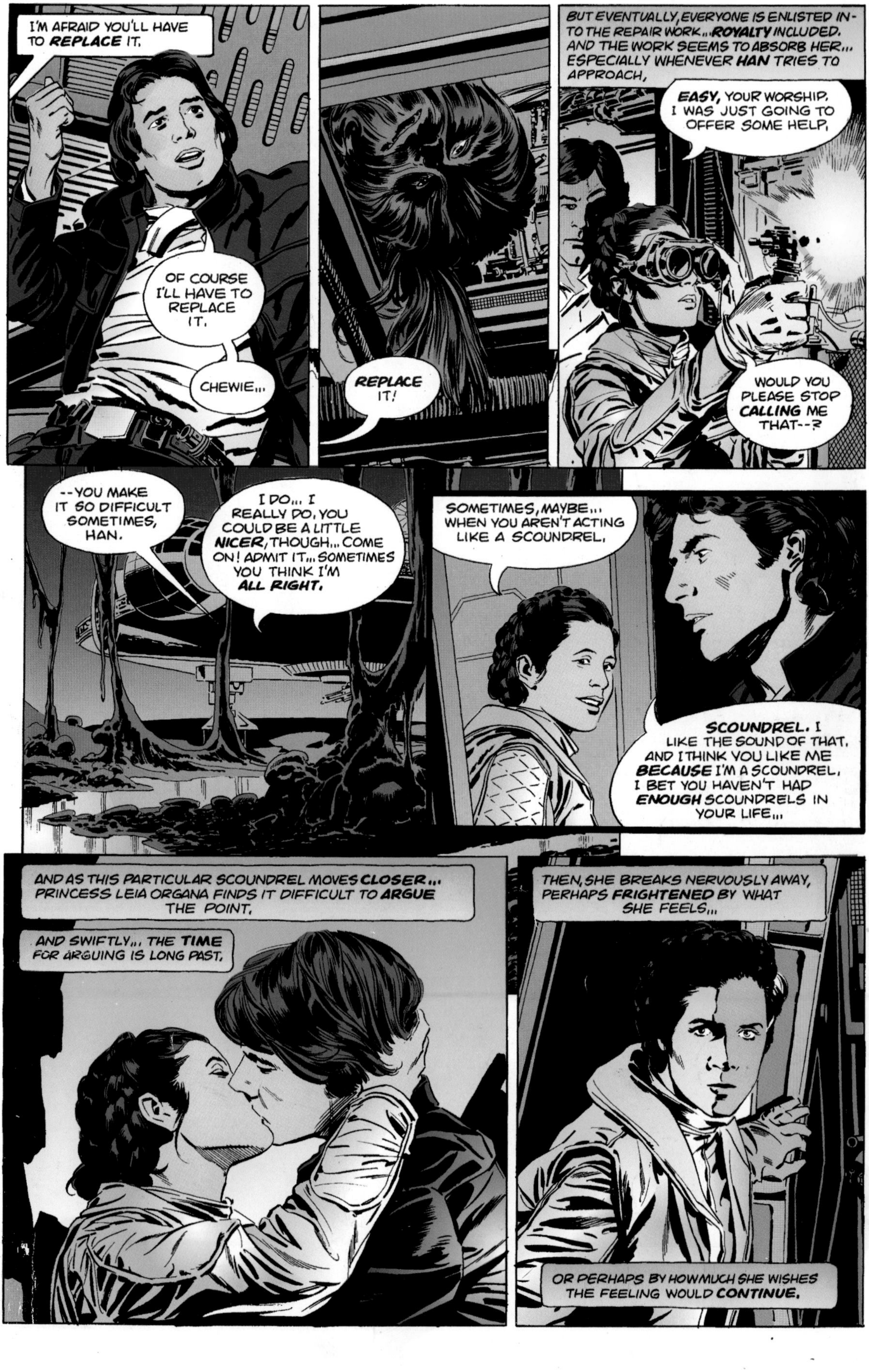
I'M AFRAID YOU'LL HAVE TO REPLACE IT.
OF COURSE I'LL HAVE TO REPLACE IT.
CHEWIE...
REPLACE IT!
BUT EVENTUALLY, EVERYONE IS ENLISTED INTO THE REPAIR WORK... ROYALTY INCLUDED. AND THE WORK SEEMS TO ABSORB HER... ESPECIALLY WHENEVER HAN TRIES TO APPROACH.
EASY, YOUR WORSHIP. I WAS JUST GOING TO OFFER SOME HELP.
WOULD YOU PLEASE STOP CALLING ME THAT--?
--YOU MAKE IT SO DIFFICULT SOMETIMES, HAN.
I DO... I REALLY DO. YOU COULD BE A LITTLE NICER, THOUGH... COME ON! ADMIT IT... SOMETIMES YOU THINK I'M ALL RIGHT.
SOMETIMES, MAYBE... WHEN YOU AREN'T ACTING LIKE A SCOUNDREL.
SCOUNDREL. I LIKE THE SOUND OF THAT. AND I THINK YOU LIKE ME BECAUSE I'M A SCOUNDREL. I BET YOU HAVEN'T HAD ENOUGH SCOUNDRELS IN YOUR LIFE...
AND AS THIS PARTICULAR SCOUNDREL MOVES CLOSER... PRINCESS LEIA ORGANA FINDS IT DIFFICULT TO ARGUE THE POINT.
AND SWIFTLY... THE TIME FOR ARGUING IS LONG PAST.
THEN, SHE BREAKS NERVOUSLY AWAY, PERHAPS FRIGHTENED BY WHAT SHE FEELS...
OR PERHAPS BY HOW MUCH SHE WISHES THE FEELING WOULD CONTINUE.

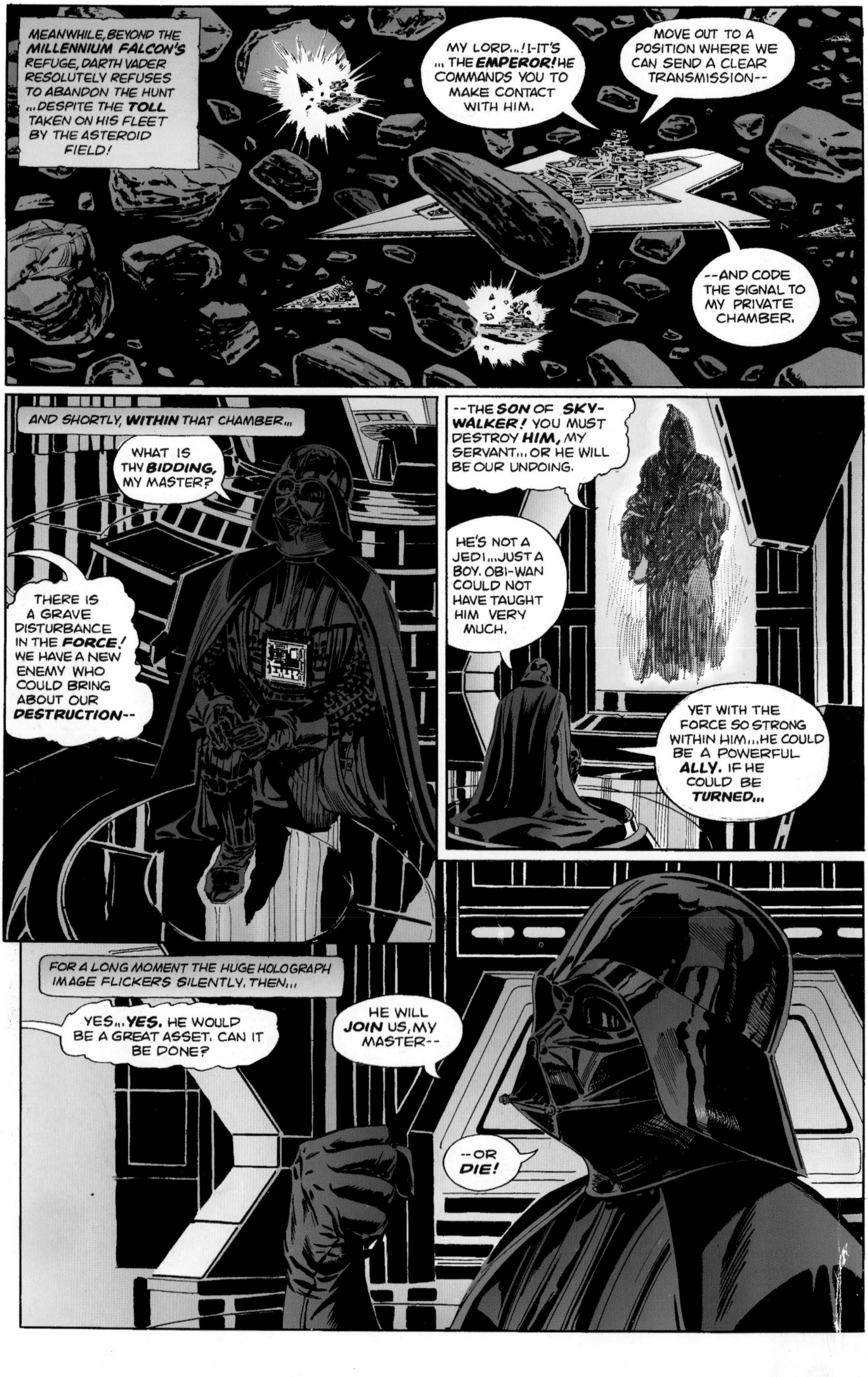

MEANWHILE, BEYOND THE MILLENNIUM FALCON'S REFUGE, DARTH VADER RESOLUTELY REFUSES TO ABANDON THE HUNT ...DESPITE THE TOLL TAKEN ON HIS FLEET BY THE ASTEROID FIELD!
MY LORD...! I-IT'S ... THE EMPEROR! HE COMMANDS YOU TO MAKE CONTACT WITH HIM.
MOVE OUT TO A POSITION WHERE WE CAN SEND A CLEAR TRANSMISSION--
--AND CODE THE SIGNAL TO MY PRIVATE CHAMBER.
AND SHORTLY, WITHIN THAT CHAMBER...
WHAT IS THY BIDDING, MY MASTER?
THERE IS A GRAVE DISTURBANCE IN THE FORCE! WE HAVE A NEW ENEMY WHO COULD BRING ABOUT OUR DESTRUCTION--
--THE SON OF SKY-WALKER! YOU MUST DESTROY HIM, MY SERVANT... OR HE WILL BE OUR UNDOING.
HE'S NOT A JEDI... JUST A BOY. OBI-WAN COULD NOT HAVE TAUGHT HIM VERY MUCH.
YET WITH THE FORCE SO STRONG WITHIN HIM... HE COULD BE A POWERFUL ALLY. IF HE COULD BE TURNED...
FOR A LONG MOMENT THE HUGE HOLOGRAPH IMAGE FLICKERS SILENTLY. THEN...
YES... YES. HE WOULD BE A GREAT ASSET. CAN IT BE DONE?
HE WILL JOIN US, MY MASTER--
--OR DIE!

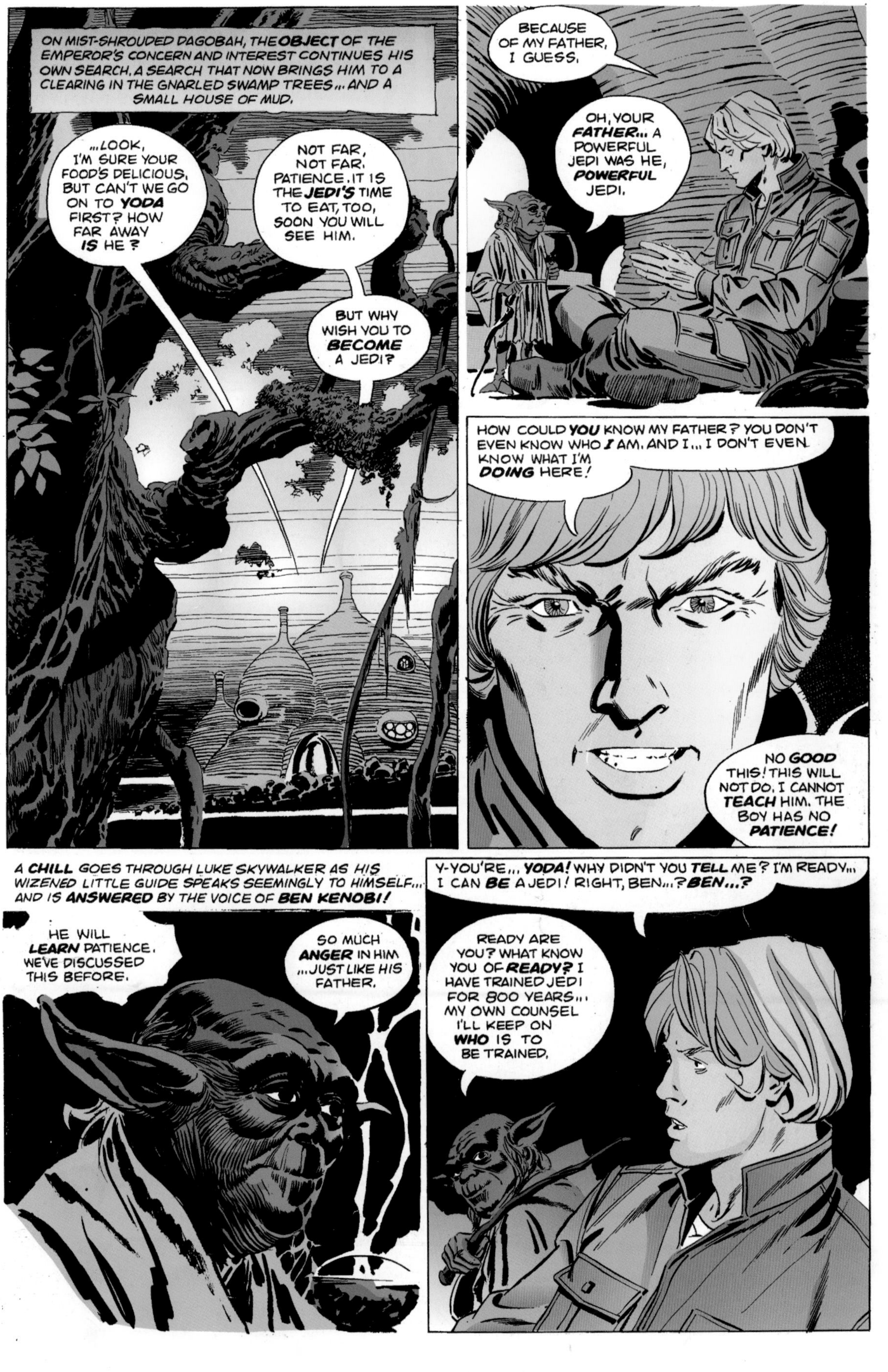

ON MIST-SHROUDED DAGOBAH, THE OBJECT OF THE EMPEROR'S CONCERN AND INTEREST CONTINUES HIS OWN SEARCH, A SEARCH THAT NOW BRINGS HIM TO A CLEARING IN THE GNARLED SWAMP TREES... AND A SMALL HOUSE OF MUD.
...LOOK, I'M SURE YOUR FOOD'S DELICIOUS, BUT CAN'T WE GO ON TO YODA FIRST? HOW FAR AWAY IS HE?
NOT FAR, NOT FAR. PATIENCE. IT IS THE JEDI'S TIME TO EAT, TOO. SOON YOU WILL SEE HIM.
BUT WHY WISH YOU TO BECOME A JEDI?
BECAUSE OF MY FATHER, I GUESS.
OH, YOUR FATHER... A POWERFUL JEDI WAS HE, POWERFUL JEDI.
HOW COULD YOU KNOW MY FATHER? YOU DON'T EVEN KNOW WHO I AM. AND I... I DON'T EVEN KNOW WHAT I'M DOING HERE!
NO GOOD THIS! THIS WILL NOT DO. I CANNOT TEACH HIM. THE BOY HAS NO PATIENCE!
A CHILL GOES THROUGH LUKE SKYWALKER AS HIS WIZENED LITTLE GUIDE SPEAKS SEEMINGLY TO HIMSELF... AND IS ANSWERED BY THE VOICE OF BEN KENOBI!
HE WILL LEARN PATIENCE. WE'VE DISCUSSED THIS BEFORE.
SO MUCH ANGER IN HIM ...JUST LIKE HIS FATHER.
Y-YOU'RE... YODA! WHY DIDN'T YOU TELL ME? I'M READY... I CAN BE A JEDI! RIGHT, BEN...? BEN...?
READY ARE YOU? WHAT KNOW YOU OF READY? I HAVE TRAINED JEDI FOR 800 YEARS... MY OWN COUNSEL I'LL KEEP ON WHO IS TO BE TRAINED.

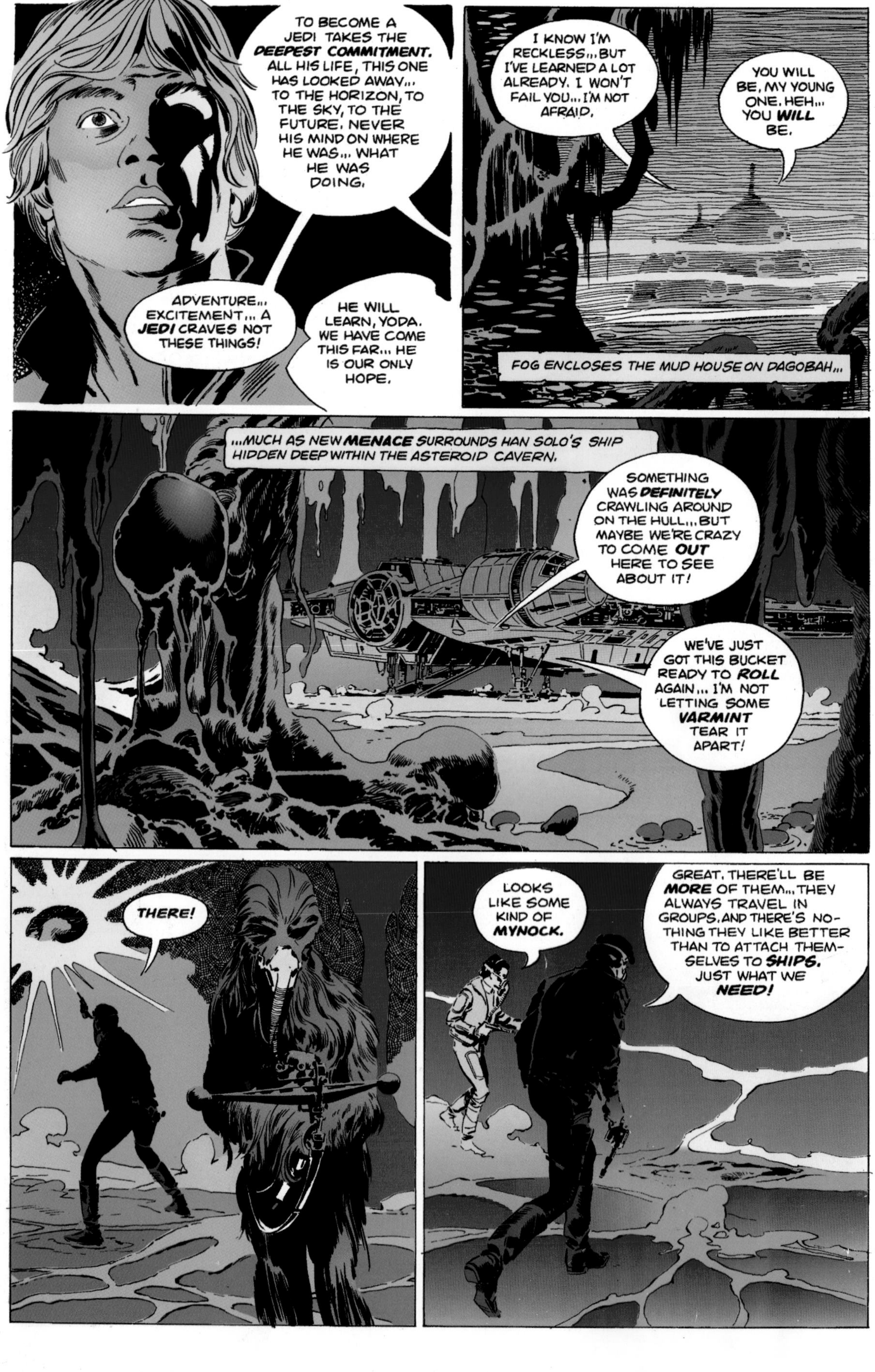
TO BECOME A JEDI TAKES THE **DEEPEST COMMITMENT.** ALL HIS LIFE, THIS ONE HAS LOOKED AWAY... TO THE HORIZON, TO THE SKY, TO THE FUTURE. NEVER HIS MIND ON WHERE HE WAS... WHAT HE WAS DOING.
ADVENTURE... EXCITEMENT... A **JEDI** CRAVES NOT THESE THINGS!
HE WILL LEARN, YODA. WE HAVE COME THIS FAR... HE IS OUR ONLY HOPE.
I KNOW I'M RECKLESS... BUT I'VE LEARNED A LOT ALREADY. I WON'T FAIL YOU... I'M NOT AFRAID.
YOU WILL BE, MY YOUNG ONE. HEH... YOU **WILL** BE.
FOG ENCLOSES THE MUD HOUSE ON DAGOBAH...
...MUCH AS NEW **MENACE** SURROUNDS HAN SOLO'S SHIP HIDDEN DEEP WITHIN THE ASTEROID CAVERN.
SOMETHING WAS **DEFINITELY** CRAWLING AROUND ON THE HULL... BUT MAYBE WE'RE CRAZY TO COME **OUT** HERE TO SEE ABOUT IT!
WE'VE JUST GOT THIS BUCKET READY TO **ROLL** AGAIN... I'M NOT LETTING SOME **VARMINT** TEAR IT APART!
THERE!
LOOKS LIKE SOME KIND OF **MYNOCK.**
GREAT. THERE'LL BE **MORE** OF THEM... THEY ALWAYS TRAVEL IN GROUPS. AND THERE'S NOTHING THEY LIKE BETTER THAN TO ATTACH THEMSELVES TO **SHIPS.** JUST WHAT WE **NEED!**

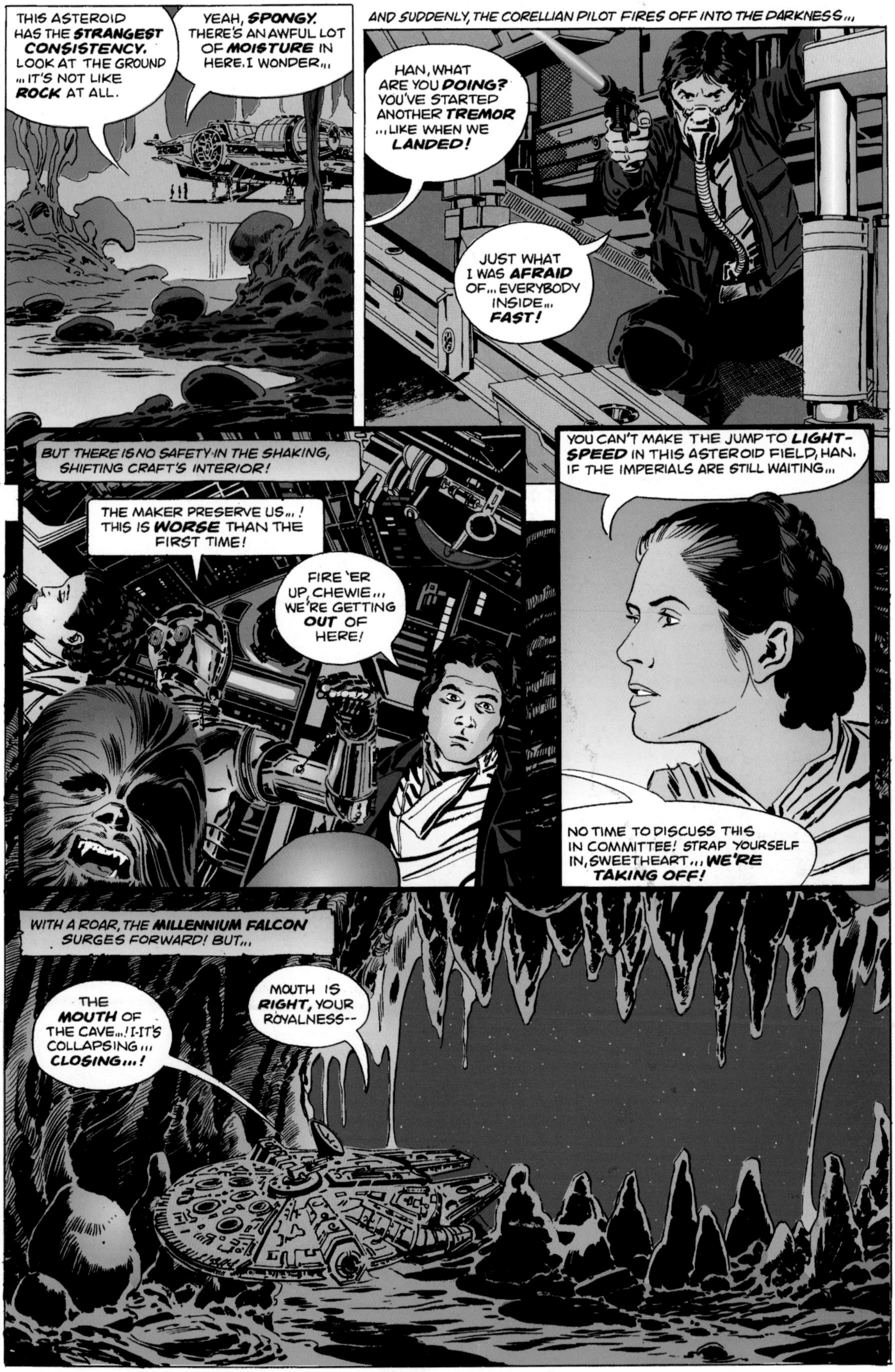
THIS ASTEROID HAS THE STRANGEST CONSISTENCY. LOOK AT THE GROUND ... IT'S NOT LIKE ROCK AT ALL.
YEAH, SPONGY. THERE'S AN AWFUL LOT OF MOISTURE IN HERE. I WONDER...
AND SUDDENLY, THE CORELLIAN PILOT FIRES OFF INTO THE DARKNESS...
HAN, WHAT ARE YOU DOING? YOU'VE STARTED ANOTHER TREMOR ... LIKE WHEN WE LANDED!
JUST WHAT I WAS AFRAID OF... EVERYBODY INSIDE... FAST!
BUT THERE IS NO SAFETY IN THE SHAKING, SHIFTING CRAFT'S INTERIOR!
THE MAKER PRESERVE US...! THIS IS WORSE THAN THE FIRST TIME!
FIRE 'ER UP, CHEWIE... WE'RE GETTING OUT OF HERE!
YOU CAN'T MAKE THE JUMP TO LIGHT-SPEED IN THIS ASTEROID FIELD, HAN. IF THE IMPERIALS ARE STILL WAITING...
NO TIME TO DISCUSS THIS IN COMMITTEE! STRAP YOURSELF IN, SWEETHEART... WE'RE TAKING OFF!
WITH A ROAR, THE MILLENNIUM FALCON SURGES FORWARD! BUT...
THE MOUTH OF THE CAVE...! I-IT'S COLLAPSING... CLOSING...!
MOUTH IS RIGHT, YOUR ROYALNESS--

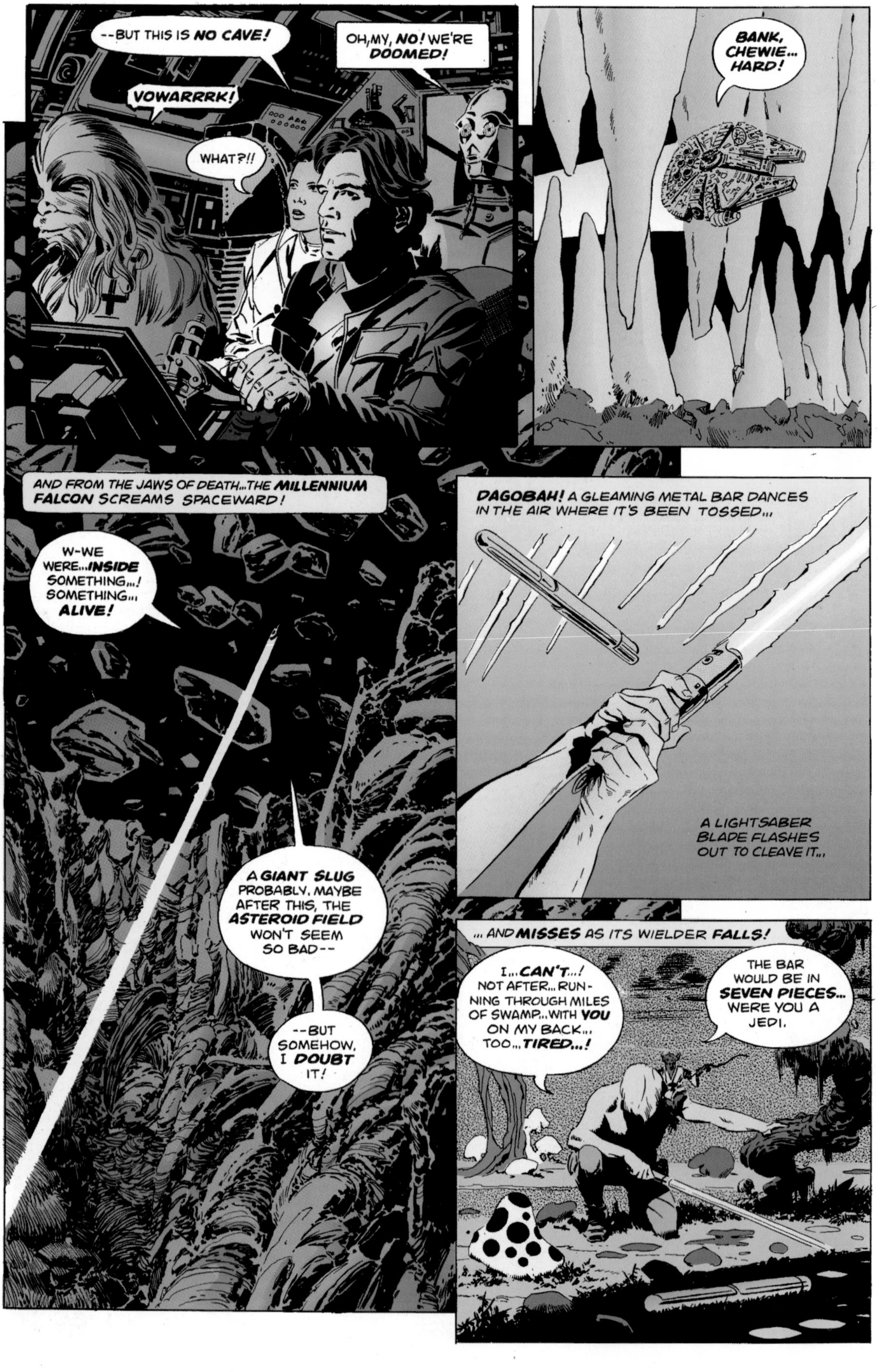

--BUT THIS IS NO CAVE!
OH, MY, NO! WE'RE DOOMED!
VOWARRRK!
WHAT?!!
BANK, CHEWIE... HARD!
AND FROM THE JAWS OF DEATH...THE MILLENNIUM FALCON SCREAMS SPACEWARD!
W-WE WERE...INSIDE SOMETHING...! SOMETHING... ALIVE!
A GIANT SLUG PROBABLY. MAYBE AFTER THIS, THE ASTEROID FIELD WON'T SEEM SO BAD--
--BUT SOMEHOW, I DOUBT IT!
DAGOBAH! A GLEAMING METAL BAR DANCES IN THE AIR WHERE IT'S BEEN TOSSED...
A LIGHTSABER BLADE FLASHES OUT TO CLEAVE IT...
...AND MISSES AS ITS WIELDER FALLS!
I...CAN'T...! NOT AFTER...RUNNING THROUGH MILES OF SWAMP...WITH YOU ON MY BACK... TOO...TIRED...!
THE BAR WOULD BE IN SEVEN PIECES... WERE YOU A JEDI.

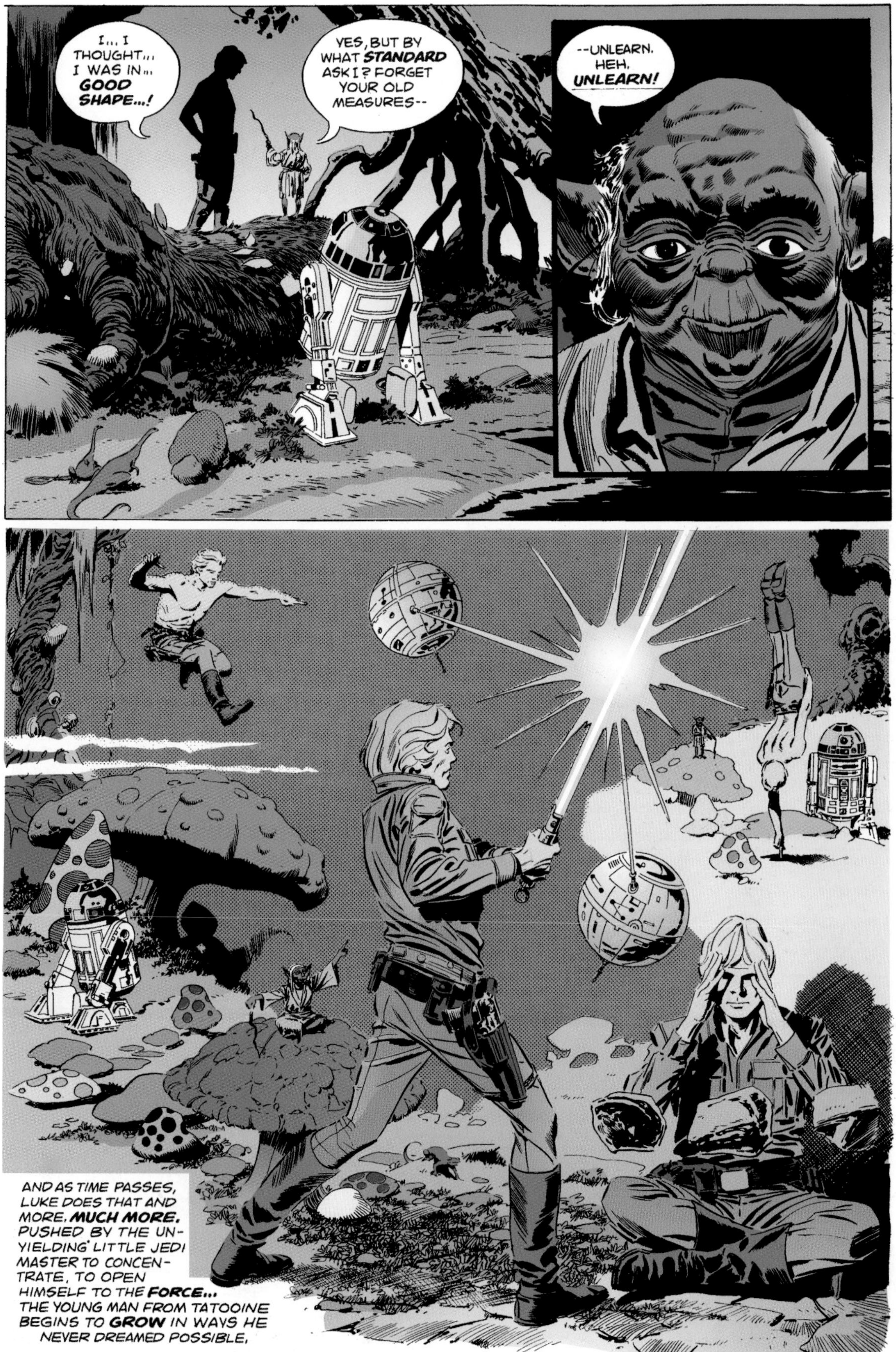
I... I THOUGHT... I WAS IN... GOOD SHAPE...!
YES, BUT BY WHAT STANDARD ASK I? FORGET YOUR OLD MEASURES--
--UNLEARN. HEH. UNLEARN!
AND AS TIME PASSES, LUKE DOES THAT AND MORE. MUCH MORE. PUSHED BY THE UNYIELDING LITTLE JEDI MASTER TO CONCENTRATE, TO OPEN HIMSELF TO THE FORCE... THE YOUNG MAN FROM TATOOINE BEGINS TO GROW IN WAYS HE NEVER DREAMED POSSIBLE.

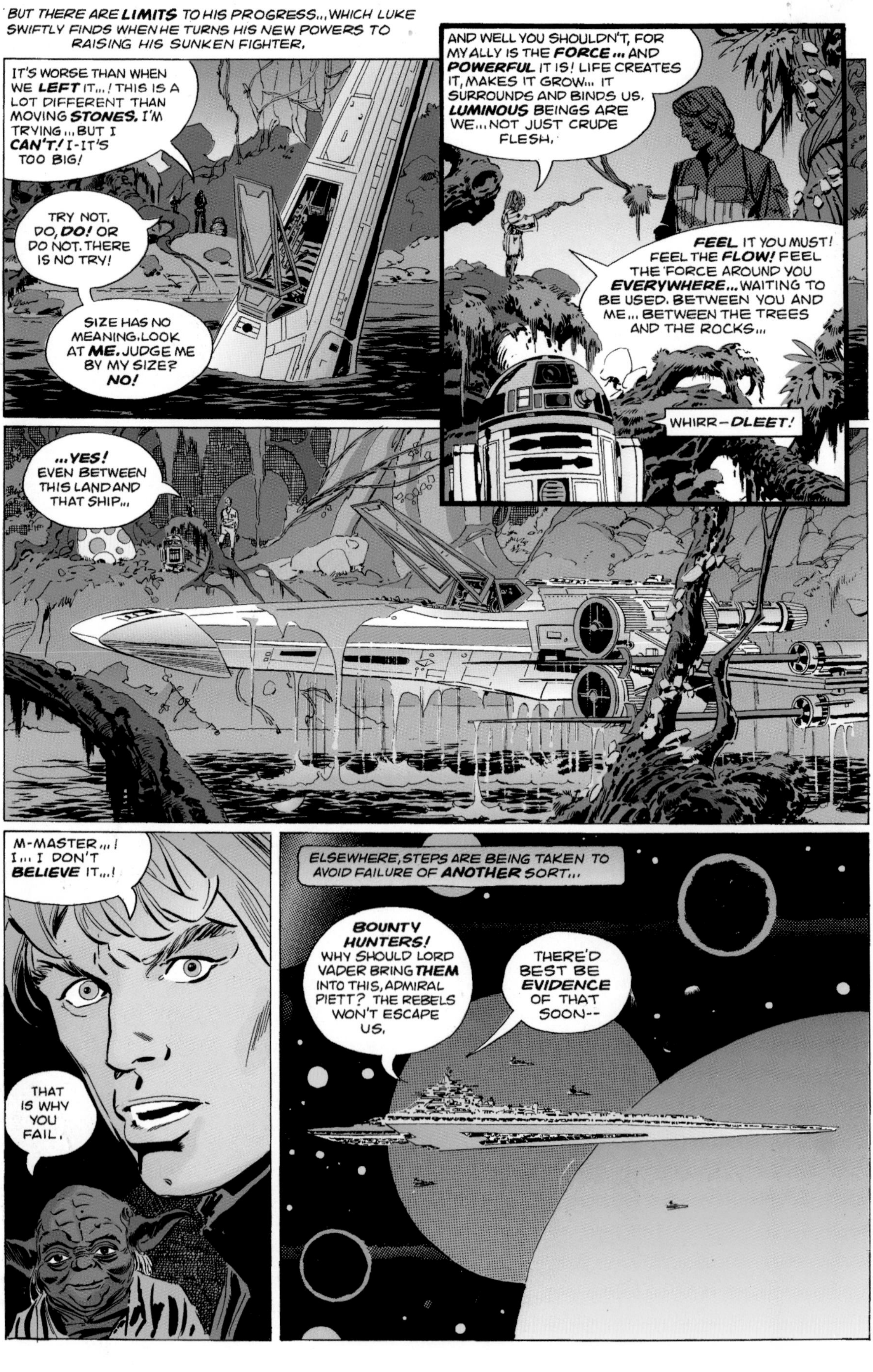

BUT THERE ARE LIMITS TO HIS PROGRESS... WHICH LUKE SWIFTLY FINDS WHEN HE TURNS HIS NEW POWERS TO RAISING HIS SUNKEN FIGHTER.
IT'S WORSE THAN WHEN WE LEFT IT...! THIS IS A LOT DIFFERENT THAN MOVING STONES. I'M TRYING... BUT I CAN'T! I-IT'S TOO BIG!
TRY NOT. DO, DO! OR DO NOT. THERE IS NO TRY!
SIZE HAS NO MEANING. LOOK AT ME. JUDGE ME BY MY SIZE? NO!
AND WELL YOU SHOULDN'T, FOR MY ALLY IS THE FORCE... AND POWERFUL IT IS! LIFE CREATES IT, MAKES IT GROW... IT SURROUNDS AND BINDS US. LUMINOUS BEINGS ARE WE... NOT JUST CRUDE FLESH.
FEEL IT YOU MUST! FEEL THE FLOW! FEEL THE FORCE AROUND YOU EVERYWHERE... WAITING TO BE USED. BETWEEN YOU AND ME... BETWEEN THE TREES AND THE ROCKS...
WHIRR-DLEET!
...YES! EVEN BETWEEN THIS LAND AND THAT SHIP...
M-MASTER...! I... I DON'T BELIEVE IT...!
THAT IS WHY YOU FAIL.
ELSEWHERE, STEPS ARE BEING TAKEN TO AVOID FAILURE OF ANOTHER SORT...
BOUNTY HUNTERS! WHY SHOULD LORD VADER BRING THEM INTO THIS, ADMIRAL PIETT? THE REBELS WON'T ESCAPE US.
THERE'D BEST BE EVIDENCE OF THAT SOON--

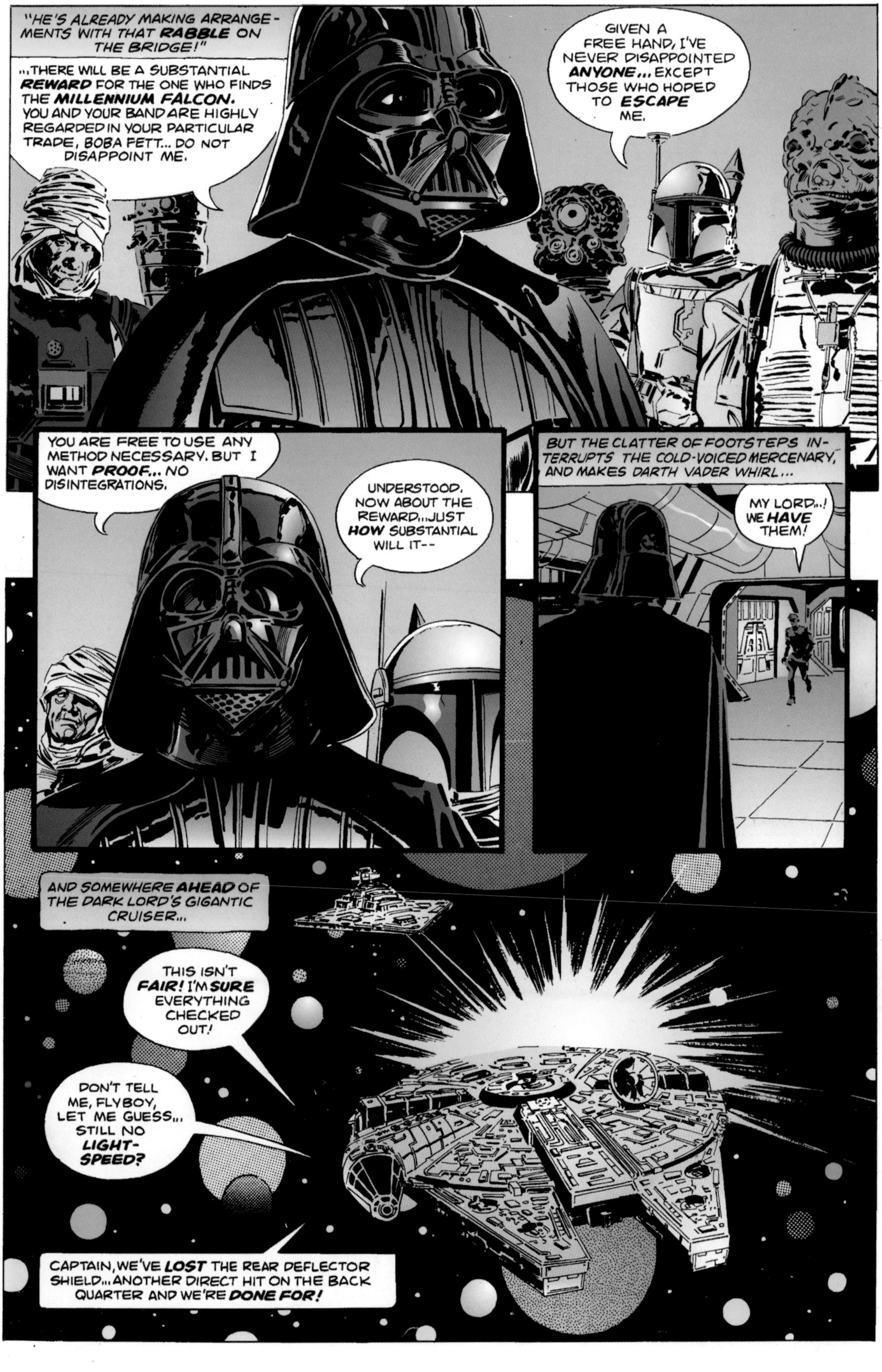
"HE'S ALREADY MAKING ARRANGEMENTS WITH THAT RABBLE ON THE BRIDGE!"
...THERE WILL BE A SUBSTANTIAL REWARD FOR THE ONE WHO FINDS THE MILLENNIUM FALCON. YOU AND YOUR BAND ARE HIGHLY REGARDED IN YOUR PARTICULAR TRADE, BOBA FETT... DO NOT DISAPPOINT ME.
GIVEN A FREE HAND, I'VE NEVER DISAPPOINTED ANYONE... EXCEPT THOSE WHO HOPED TO ESCAPE ME.
YOU ARE FREE TO USE ANY METHOD NECESSARY. BUT I WANT PROOF... NO DISINTEGRATIONS.
UNDERSTOOD. NOW ABOUT THE REWARD... JUST HOW SUBSTANTIAL WILL IT--
BUT THE CLATTER OF FOOTSTEPS INTERRUPTS THE COLD-VOICED MERCENARY, AND MAKES DARTH VADER WHIRL...
MY LORD...! WE HAVE THEM!
AND SOMEWHERE AHEAD OF THE DARK LORD'S GIGANTIC CRUISER...
THIS ISN'T FAIR! I'M SURE EVERYTHING CHECKED OUT!
DON'T TELL ME, FLYBOY, LET ME GUESS... STILL NO LIGHT-SPEED?
CAPTAIN, WE'VE LOST THE REAR DEFLECTOR SHIELD... ANOTHER DIRECT HIT ON THE BACK QUARTER AND WE'RE DONE FOR!

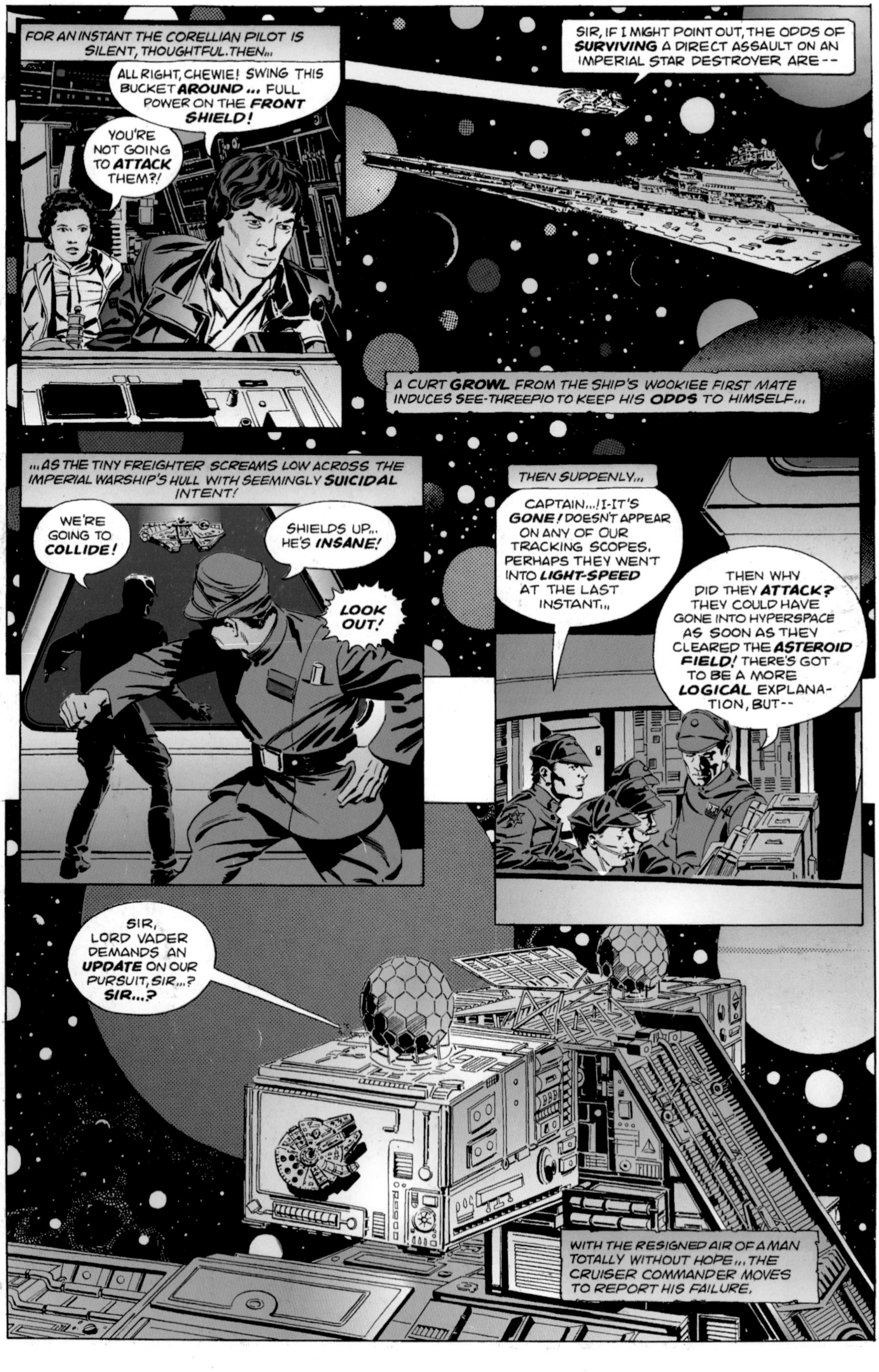
FOR AN INSTANT THE CORELLIAN PILOT IS SILENT, THOUGHTFUL. THEN...
ALL RIGHT, CHEWIE! SWING THIS BUCKET AROUND... FULL POWER ON THE FRONT SHIELD!
YOU'RE NOT GOING TO ATTACK THEM?!
SIR, IF I MIGHT POINT OUT, THE ODDS OF SURVIVING A DIRECT ASSAULT ON AN IMPERIAL STAR DESTROYER ARE--
A CURT GROWL FROM THE SHIP'S WOOKIEE FIRST MATE INDUCES SEE-THREEPIO TO KEEP HIS ODDS TO HIMSELF...
...AS THE TINY FREIGHTER SCREAMS LOW ACROSS THE IMPERIAL WARSHIP'S HULL WITH SEEMINGLY SUICIDAL INTENT!
WE'RE GOING TO COLLIDE!
SHIELDS UP... HE'S INSANE!
LOOK OUT!
THEN SUDDENLY...
CAPTAIN...! I-IT'S GONE! DOESN'T APPEAR ON ANY OF OUR TRACKING SCOPES. PERHAPS THEY WENT INTO LIGHT-SPEED AT THE LAST INSTANT...
THEN WHY DID THEY ATTACK? THEY COULD HAVE GONE INTO HYPERSPACE AS SOON AS THEY CLEARED THE ASTEROID FIELD! THERE'S GOT TO BE A MORE LOGICAL EXPLANATION, BUT--
SIR, LORD VADER DEMANDS AN UPDATE ON OUR PURSUIT, SIR...? SIR...?
WITH THE RESIGNED AIR OF A MAN TOTALLY WITHOUT HOPE... THE CRUISER COMMANDER MOVES TO REPORT HIS FAILURE.

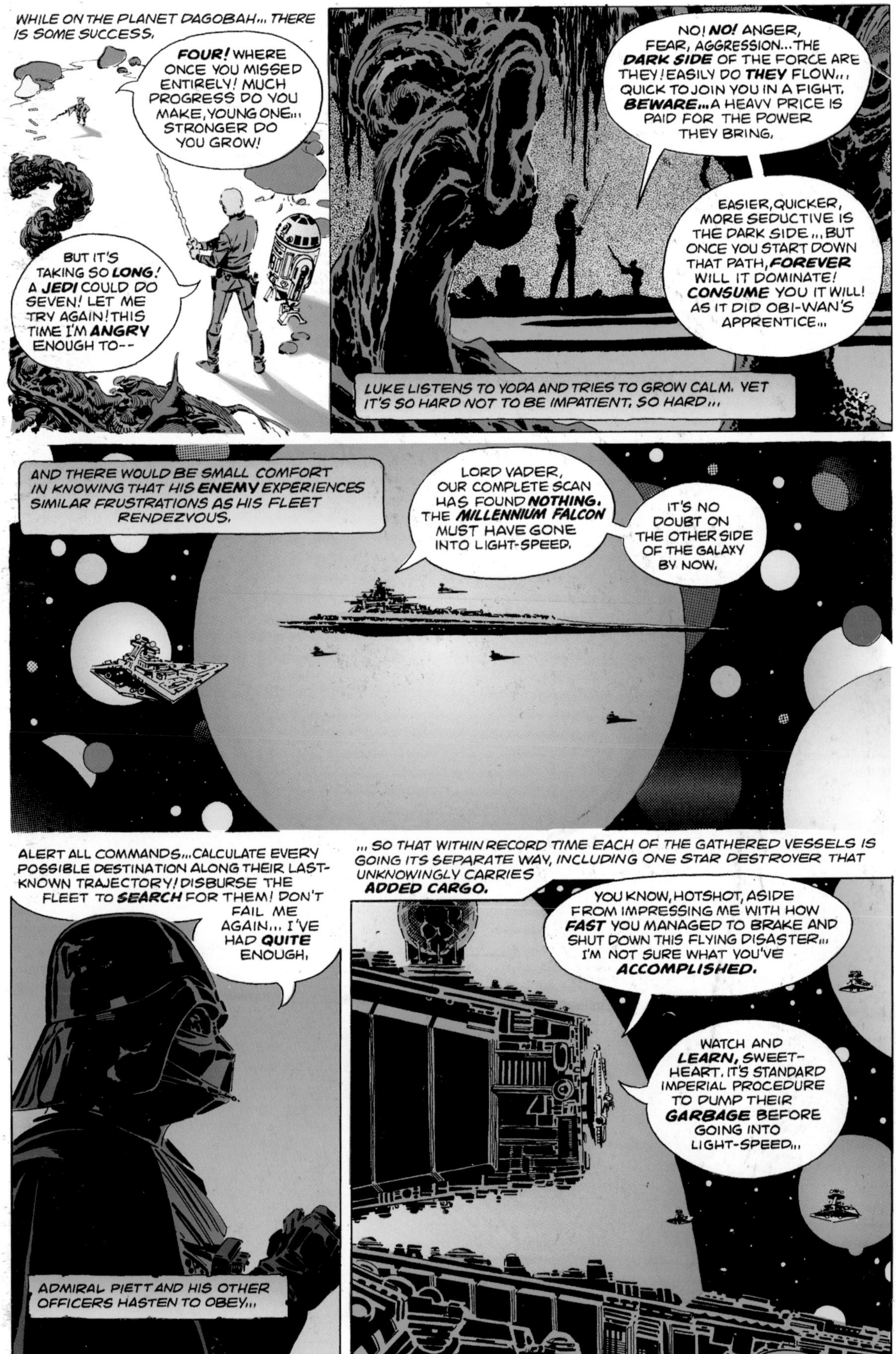
WHILE ON THE PLANET DAGOBAH... THERE IS SOME SUCCESS.
FOUR! WHERE ONCE YOU MISSED ENTIRELY! MUCH PROGRESS DO YOU MAKE, YOUNG ONE... STRONGER DO YOU GROW!
BUT IT'S TAKING SO LONG! A JEDI COULD DO SEVEN! LET ME TRY AGAIN! THIS TIME I'M ANGRY ENOUGH TO--
NO! NO! ANGER, FEAR, AGGRESSION... THE DARK SIDE OF THE FORCE ARE THEY! EASILY DO THEY FLOW... QUICK TO JOIN YOU IN A FIGHT. BEWARE... A HEAVY PRICE IS PAID FOR THE POWER THEY BRING.
EASIER, QUICKER, MORE SEDUCTIVE IS THE DARK SIDE... BUT ONCE YOU START DOWN THAT PATH, FOREVER WILL IT DOMINATE! CONSUME YOU IT WILL! AS IT DID OBI-WAN'S APPRENTICE...
LUKE LISTENS TO YODA AND TRIES TO GROW CALM. YET IT'S SO HARD NOT TO BE IMPATIENT. SO HARD...
AND THERE WOULD BE SMALL COMFORT IN KNOWING THAT HIS ENEMY EXPERIENCES SIMILAR FRUSTRATIONS AS HIS FLEET RENDEZVOUS.
LORD VADER, OUR COMPLETE SCAN HAS FOUND NOTHING. THE MILLENNIUM FALCON MUST HAVE GONE INTO LIGHT-SPEED.
IT'S NO DOUBT ON THE OTHER SIDE OF THE GALAXY BY NOW.
ALERT ALL COMMANDS... CALCULATE EVERY POSSIBLE DESTINATION ALONG THEIR LAST-KNOWN TRAJECTORY! DISBURSE THE FLEET TO SEARCH FOR THEM! DON'T FAIL ME AGAIN... I'VE HAD QUITE ENOUGH.
ADMIRAL PIETT AND HIS OTHER OFFICERS HASTEN TO OBEY...
... SO THAT WITHIN RECORD TIME EACH OF THE GATHERED VESSELS IS GOING ITS SEPARATE WAY, INCLUDING ONE STAR DESTROYER THAT UNKNOWINGLY CARRIES ADDED CARGO.
YOU KNOW, HOTSHOT, ASIDE FROM IMPRESSING ME WITH HOW FAST YOU MANAGED TO BRAKE AND SHUT DOWN THIS FLYING DISASTER... I'M NOT SURE WHAT YOU'VE ACCOMPLISHED.
WATCH AND LEARN, SWEET-HEART. IT'S STANDARD IMPERIAL PROCEDURE TO DUMP THEIR GARBAGE BEFORE GOING INTO LIGHT-SPEED...

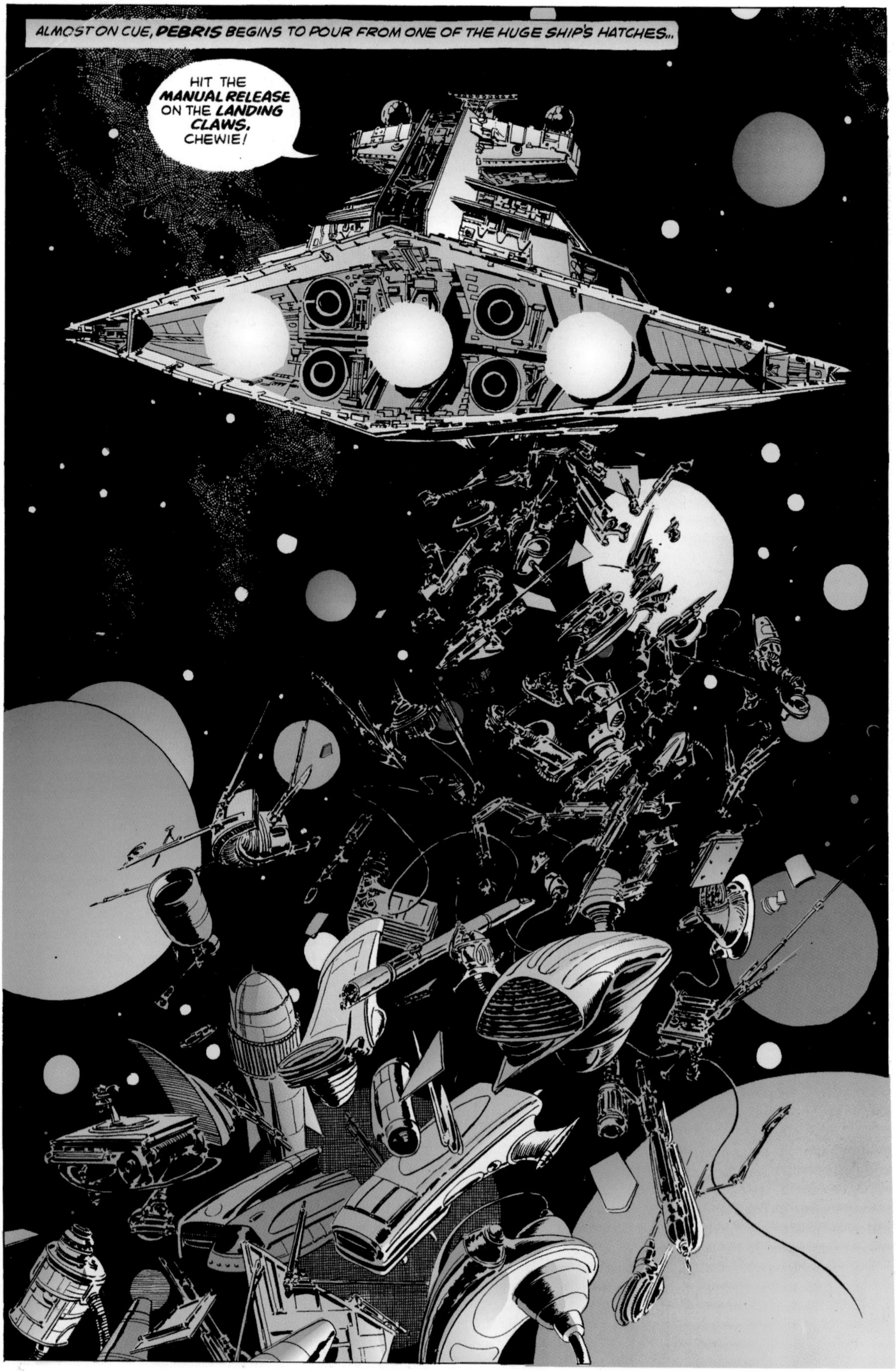
ALMOST ON CUE, DEBRIS BEGINS TO POUR FROM ONE OF THE HUGE SHIP'S HATCHES...
HIT THE MANUAL RELEASE ON THE LANDING CLAWS, CHEWIE!

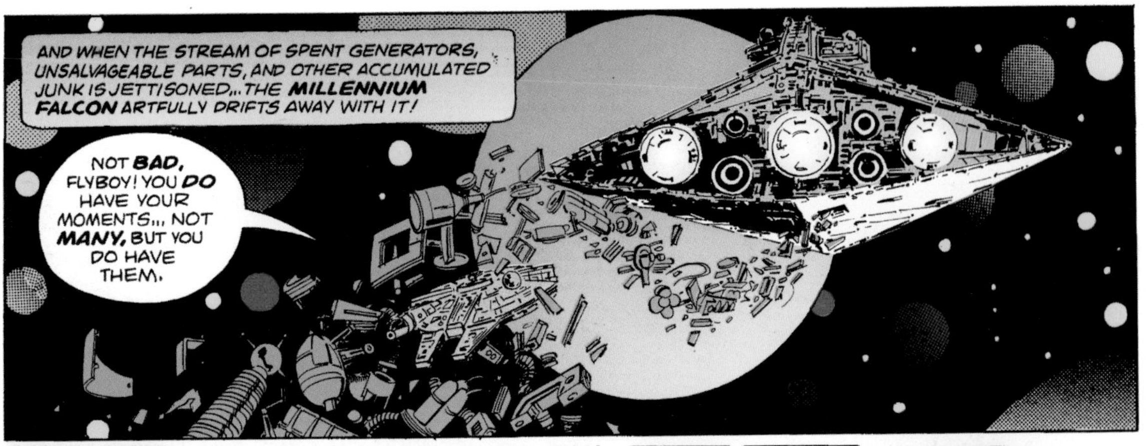
AND WHEN THE STREAM OF SPENT GENERATORS, UNSALVAGEABLE PARTS, AND OTHER ACCUMULATED JUNK IS JETTISONED... THE MILLENNIUM FALCON ARTFULLY DRIFTS AWAY WITH IT!
NOT BAD, FLYBOY! YOU DO HAVE YOUR MOMENTS... NOT MANY, BUT YOU DO HAVE THEM.

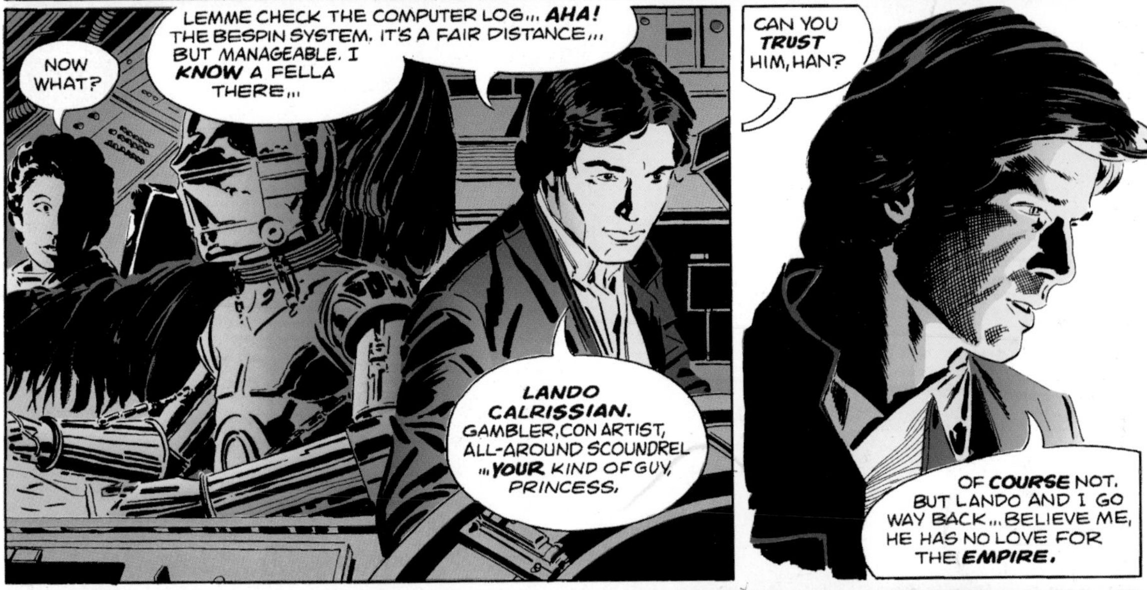
NOW WHAT?
LEMME CHECK THE COMPUTER LOG... AHA! THE BESPIN SYSTEM. IT'S A FAIR DISTANCE... BUT MANAGEABLE. I KNOW A FELLA THERE...
LANDO CALRISSIAN. GAMBLER, CON ARTIST, ALL-AROUND SCOUNDREL ...YOUR KIND OF GUY, PRINCESS.
CAN YOU TRUST HIM, HAN?
OF COURSE NOT. BUT LANDO AND I GO WAY BACK... BELIEVE ME, HE HAS NO LOVE FOR THE EMPIRE.

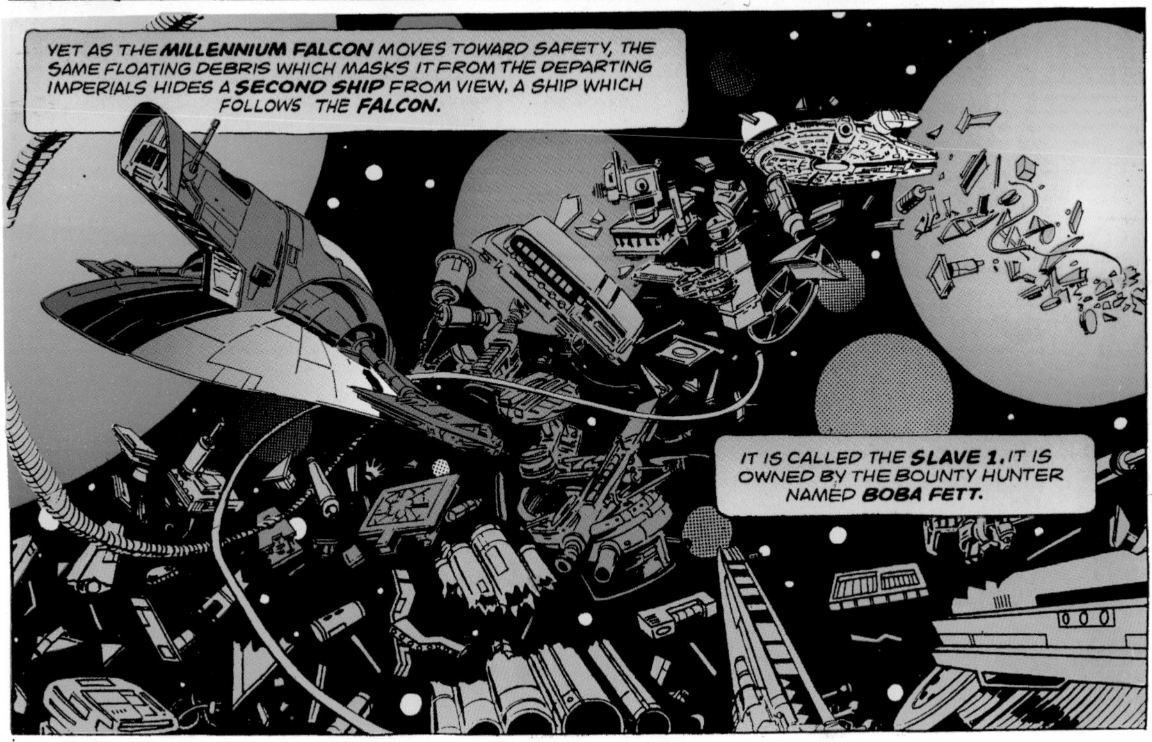
YET AS THE MILLENNIUM FALCON MOVES TOWARD SAFETY, THE SAME FLOATING DEBRIS WHICH MASKS IT FROM THE DEPARTING IMPERIALS HIDES A SECOND SHIP FROM VIEW, A SHIP WHICH FOLLOWS THE FALCON.
IT IS CALLED THE SLAVE 1. IT IS OWNED BY THE BOUNTY HUNTER NAMED BOBA FETT.

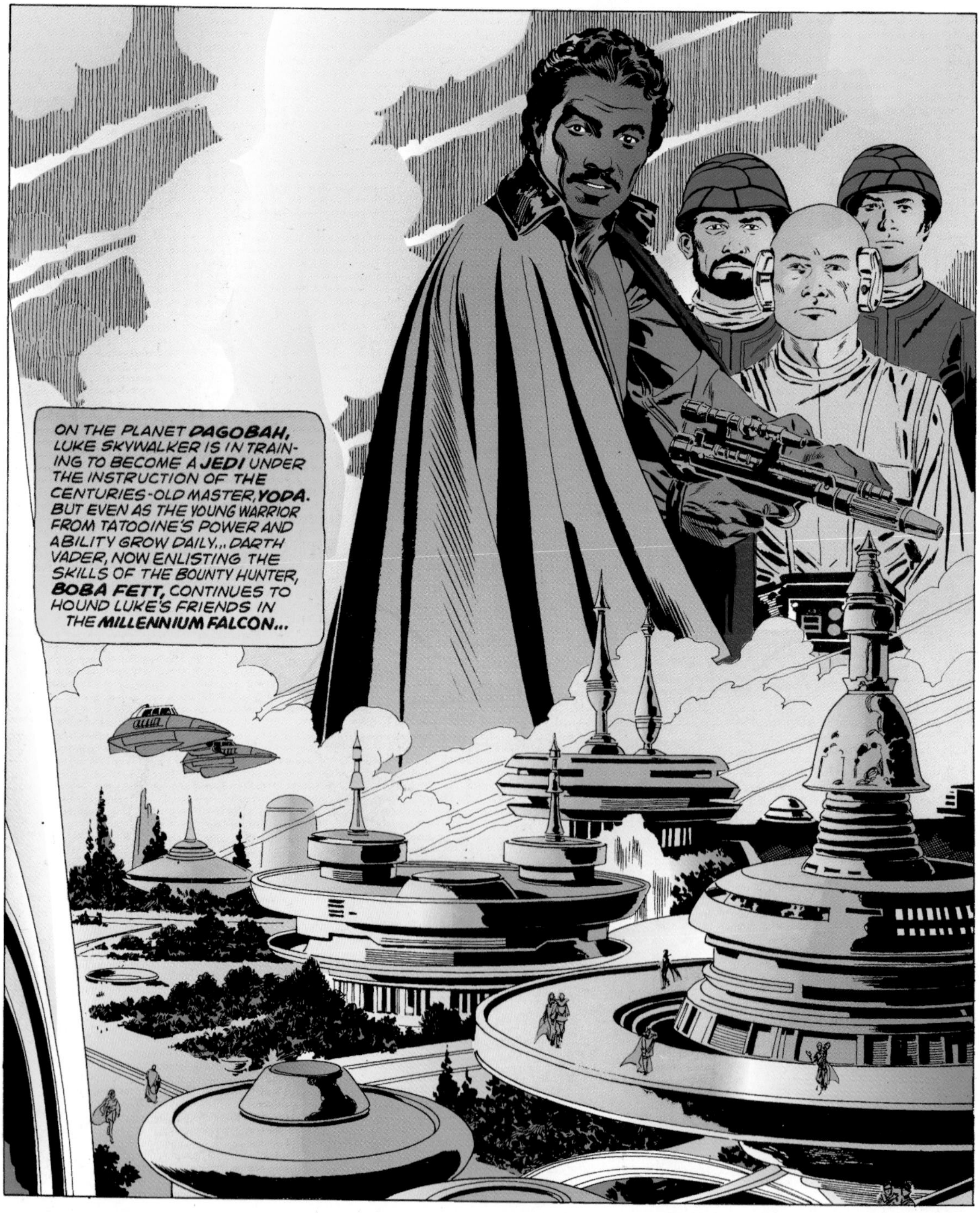
ON THE PLANET DAGOBAH, LUKE SKYWALKER IS IN TRAINING TO BECOME A JEDI UNDER THE INSTRUCTION OF THE CENTURIES-OLD MASTER, YODA. BUT EVEN AS THE YOUNG WARRIOR FROM TATOOINE'S POWER AND ABILITY GROW DAILY... DARTH VADER, NOW ENLISTING THE SKILLS OF THE BOUNTY HUNTER, BOBA FETT, CONTINUES TO HOUND LUKE'S FRIENDS IN THE MILLENNIUM FALCON...

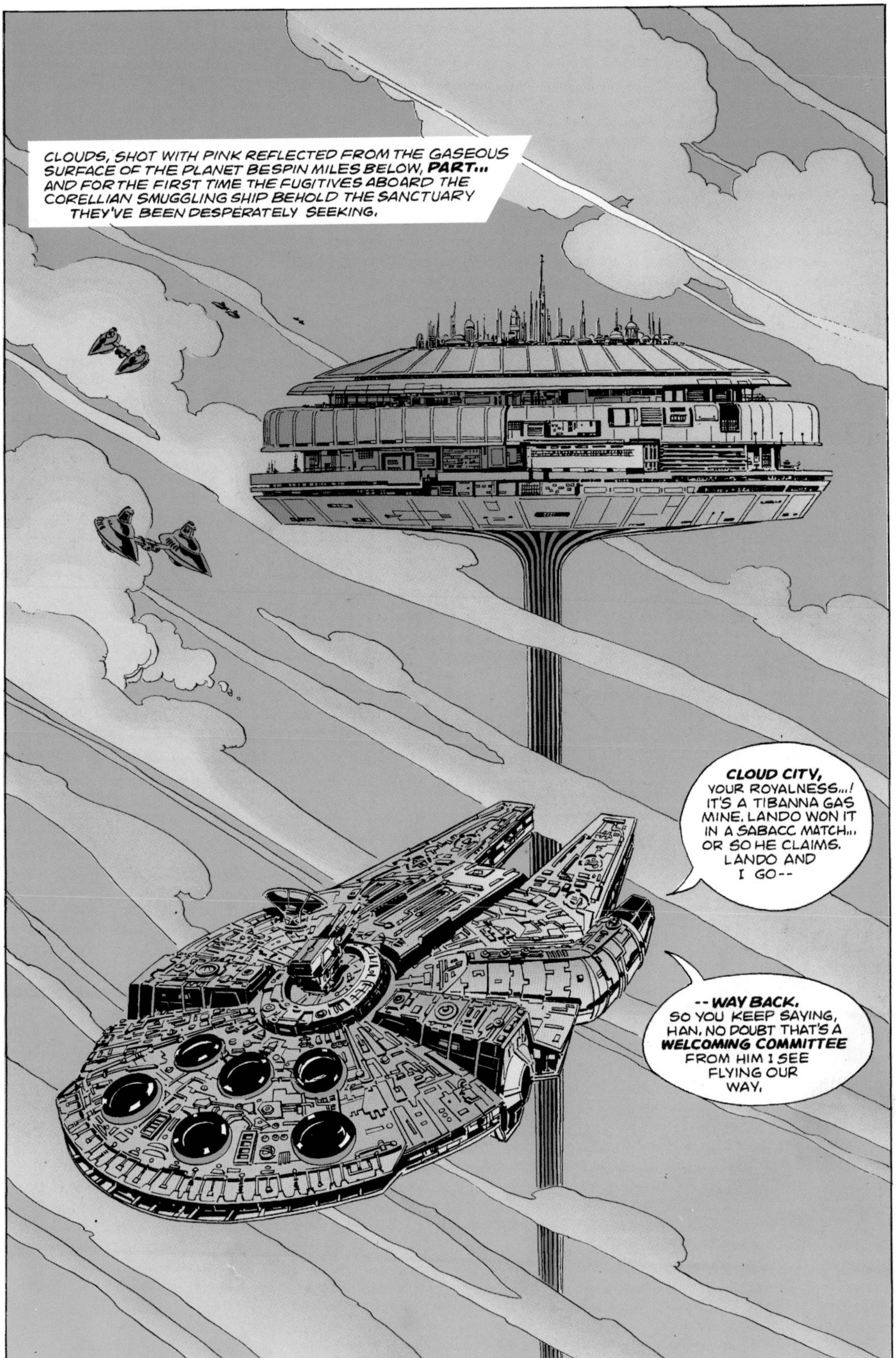
CLOUDS, SHOT WITH PINK REFLECTED FROM THE GASEOUS SURFACE OF THE PLANET BESPIN MILES BELOW, **PART...** AND FOR THE FIRST TIME THE FUGITIVES ABOARD THE CORELLIAN SMUGGLING SHIP BEHOLD THE SANCTUARY THEY'VE BEEN DESPERATELY SEEKING.
CLOUD CITY, YOUR ROYALNESS...! IT'S A TIBANNA GAS MINE. LANDO WON IT IN A SABACC MATCH... OR SO HE CLAIMS. LANDO AND I GO--
--WAY BACK. SO YOU KEEP SAYING, HAN. NO DOUBT THAT'S A **WELCOMING COMMITTEE** FROM HIM I SEE FLYING OUR WAY.

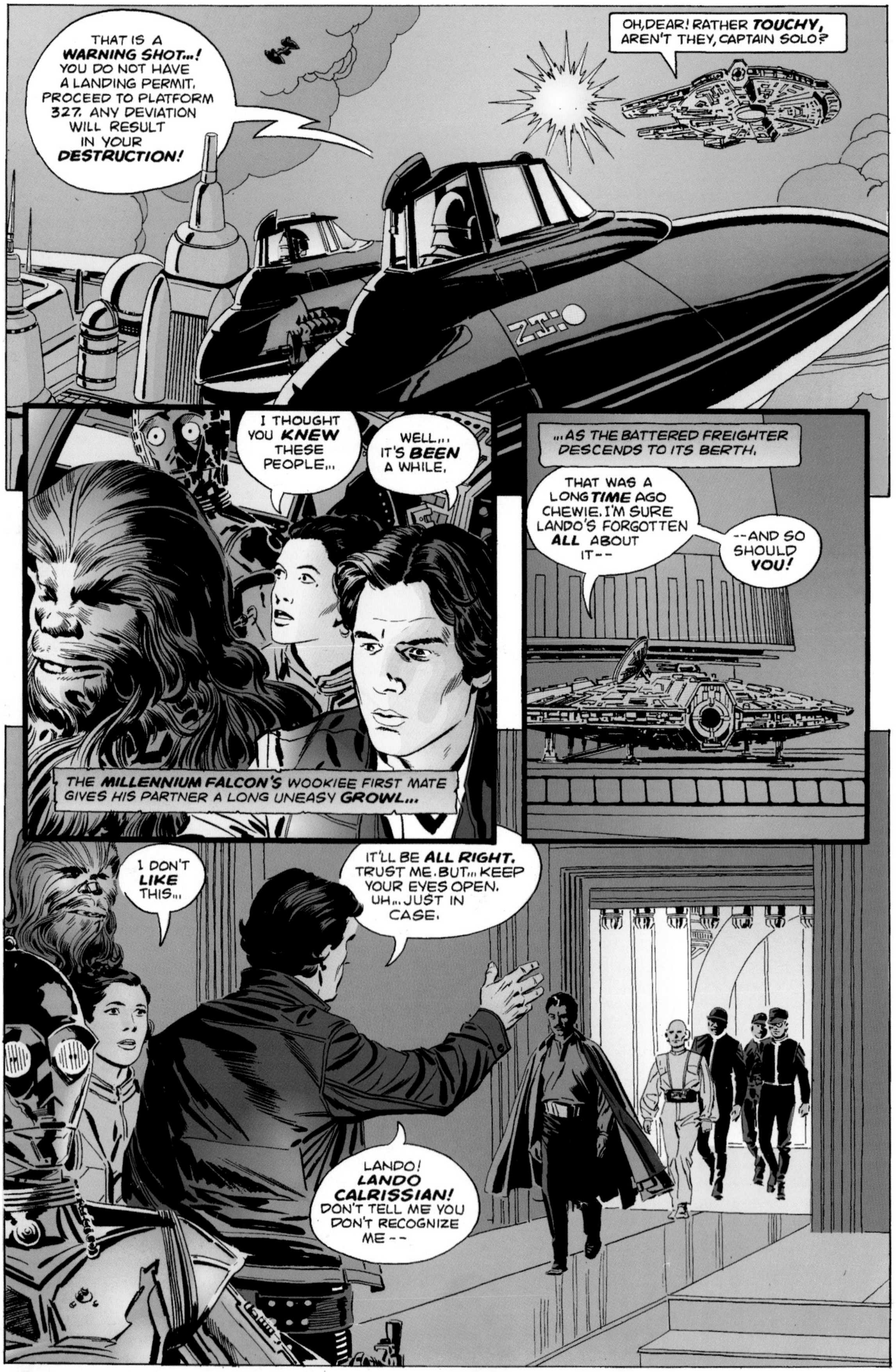
THAT IS A WARNING SHOT...! YOU DO NOT HAVE A LANDING PERMIT. PROCEED TO PLATFORM 327. ANY DEVIATION WILL RESULT IN YOUR DESTRUCTION!
OH, DEAR! RATHER TOUCHY, AREN'T THEY, CAPTAIN SOLO?
I THOUGHT YOU KNEW THESE PEOPLE...
WELL... IT'S BEEN A WHILE.
THE MILLENNIUM FALCON'S WOOKIEE FIRST MATE GIVES HIS PARTNER A LONG UNEASY GROWL...
...AS THE BATTERED FREIGHTER DESCENDS TO ITS BERTH.
THAT WAS A LONG TIME AGO CHEWIE. I'M SURE LANDO'S FORGOTTEN ALL ABOUT IT--
--AND SO SHOULD YOU!
I DON'T LIKE THIS...
IT'LL BE ALL RIGHT. TRUST ME. BUT... KEEP YOUR EYES OPEN. UH... JUST IN CASE.
LANDO! LANDO CALRISSIAN! DON'T TELL ME YOU DON'T RECOGNIZE ME--

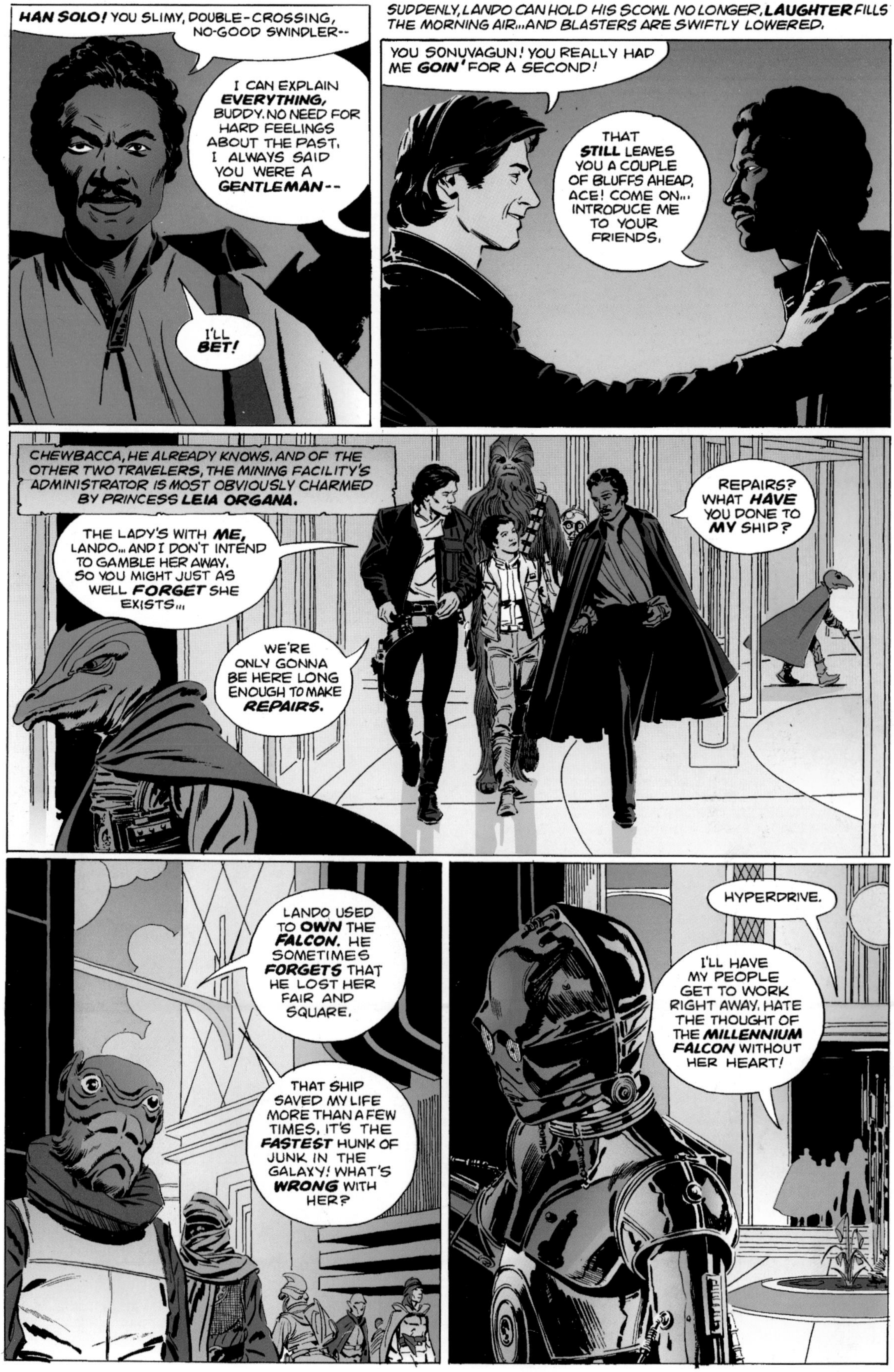
HAN SOLO! YOU SLIMY, DOUBLE-CROSSING, NO-GOOD SWINDLER--
I CAN EXPLAIN EVERYTHING, BUDDY. NO NEED FOR HARD FEELINGS ABOUT THE PAST. I ALWAYS SAID YOU WERE A GENTLEMAN--
I'LL BET!
SUDDENLY, LANDO CAN HOLD HIS SCOWL NO LONGER. LAUGHTER FILLS THE MORNING AIR... AND BLASTERS ARE SWIFTLY LOWERED.
YOU SONUVAGUN! YOU REALLY HAD ME GOIN' FOR A SECOND!
THAT STILL LEAVES YOU A COUPLE OF BLUFFS AHEAD, ACE! COME ON... INTRODUCE ME TO YOUR FRIENDS.
CHEWBACCA, HE ALREADY KNOWS. AND OF THE OTHER TWO TRAVELERS, THE MINING FACILITY'S ADMINISTRATOR IS MOST OBVIOUSLY CHARMED BY PRINCESS LEIA ORGANA.
THE LADY'S WITH ME, LANDO... AND I DON'T INTEND TO GAMBLE HER AWAY. SO YOU MIGHT JUST AS WELL FORGET SHE EXISTS...
WE'RE ONLY GONNA BE HERE LONG ENOUGH TO MAKE REPAIRS.
REPAIRS? WHAT HAVE YOU DONE TO MY SHIP?
LANDO USED TO OWN THE FALCON. HE SOMETIMES FORGETS THAT HE LOST HER FAIR AND SQUARE.
THAT SHIP SAVED MY LIFE MORE THAN A FEW TIMES. IT'S THE FASTEST HUNK OF JUNK IN THE GALAXY! WHAT'S WRONG WITH HER?
HYPERDRIVE.
I'LL HAVE MY PEOPLE GET TO WORK RIGHT AWAY. HATE THE THOUGHT OF THE MILLENNIUM FALCON WITHOUT HER HEART!

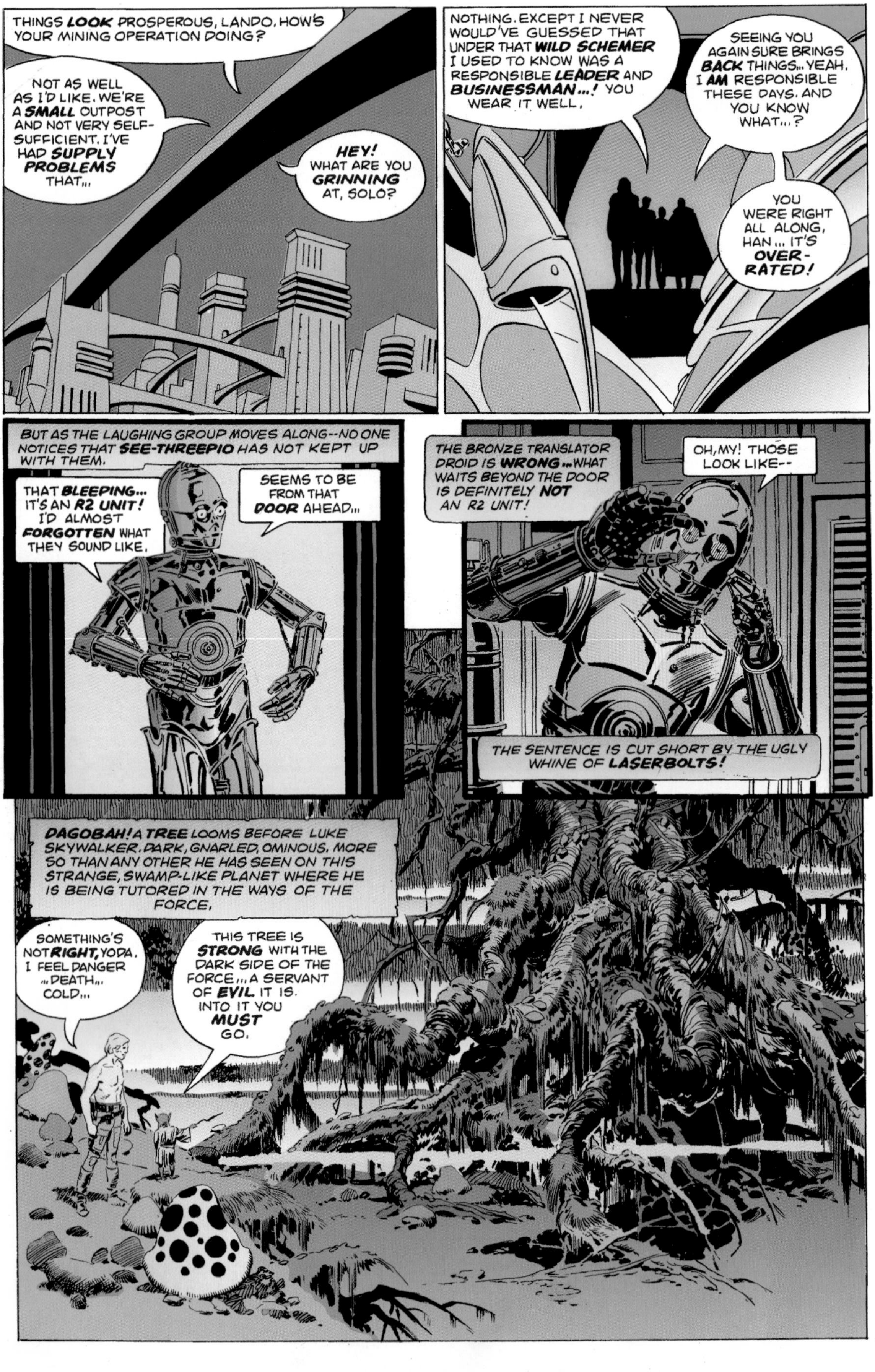
THINGS LOOK PROSPEROUS, LANDO. HOW'S YOUR MINING OPERATION DOING?
NOT AS WELL AS I'D LIKE. WE'RE A SMALL OUTPOST AND NOT VERY SELF-SUFFICIENT. I'VE HAD SUPPLY PROBLEMS THAT...
HEY! WHAT ARE YOU GRINNING AT, SOLO?
NOTHING. EXCEPT I NEVER WOULD'VE GUESSED THAT UNDER THAT WILD SCHEMER I USED TO KNOW WAS A RESPONSIBLE LEADER AND BUSINESSMAN...! YOU WEAR IT WELL.
SEEING YOU AGAIN SURE BRINGS BACK THINGS... YEAH, I AM RESPONSIBLE THESE DAYS. AND YOU KNOW WHAT...?
YOU WERE RIGHT ALL ALONG, HAN... IT'S OVER-RATED!
BUT AS THE LAUGHING GROUP MOVES ALONG--NO ONE NOTICES THAT SEE-THREEPIO HAS NOT KEPT UP WITH THEM.
THAT BLEEPING... IT'S AN R2 UNIT! I'D ALMOST FORGOTTEN WHAT THEY SOUND LIKE.
SEEMS TO BE FROM THAT DOOR AHEAD...
THE BRONZE TRANSLATOR DROID IS WRONG... WHAT WAITS BEYOND THE DOOR IS DEFINITELY NOT AN R2 UNIT!
OH, MY! THOSE LOOK LIKE--
THE SENTENCE IS CUT SHORT BY THE UGLY WHINE OF LASERBOLTS!
DAGOBAH! A TREE LOOMS BEFORE LUKE SKYWALKER. DARK, GNARLED, OMINOUS. MORE SO THAN ANY OTHER HE HAS SEEN ON THIS STRANGE, SWAMP-LIKE PLANET WHERE HE IS BEING TUTORED IN THE WAYS OF THE FORCE.
SOMETHING'S NOT RIGHT, YODA. I FEEL DANGER ...DEATH... COLD...
THIS TREE IS STRONG WITH THE DARK SIDE OF THE FORCE... A SERVANT OF EVIL IT IS. INTO IT YOU MUST GO.

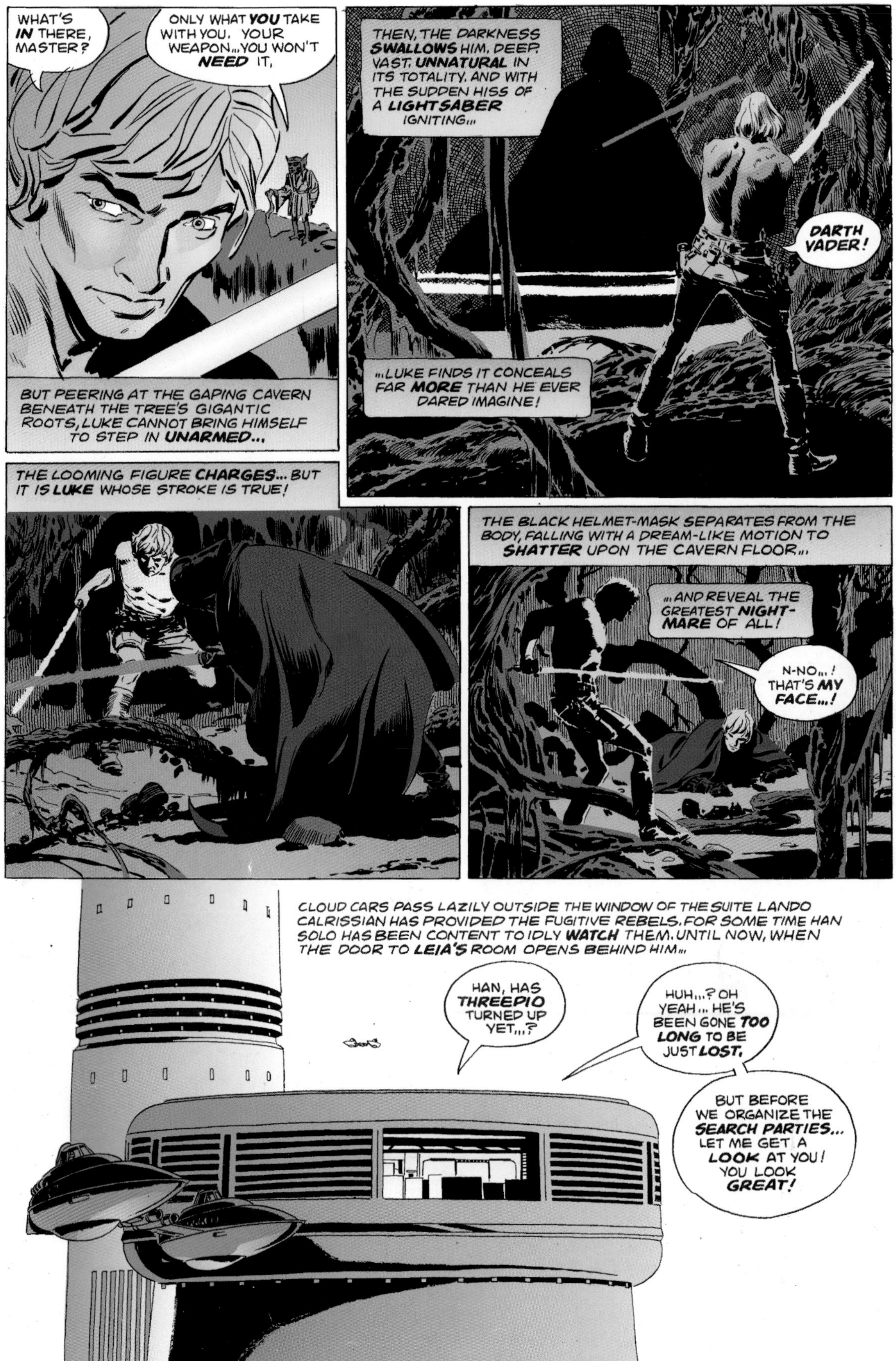
WHAT'S IN THERE, MASTER?
ONLY WHAT YOU TAKE WITH YOU. YOUR WEAPON... YOU WON'T NEED IT.
BUT PEERING AT THE GAPING CAVERN BENEATH THE TREE'S GIGANTIC ROOTS, LUKE CANNOT BRING HIMSELF TO STEP IN UNARMED...
THEN, THE DARKNESS SWALLOWS HIM. DEEP. VAST. UNNATURAL IN ITS TOTALITY. AND WITH THE SUDDEN HISS OF A LIGHTSABER IGNITING...
...LUKE FINDS IT CONCEALS FAR MORE THAN HE EVER DARED IMAGINE!
DARTH VADER!
THE LOOMING FIGURE CHARGES... BUT IT IS LUKE WHOSE STROKE IS TRUE!
THE BLACK HELMET-MASK SEPARATES FROM THE BODY, FALLING WITH A DREAM-LIKE MOTION TO SHATTER UPON THE CAVERN FLOOR...
...AND REVEAL THE GREATEST NIGHTMARE OF ALL!
N-NO...! THAT'S MY FACE...!
CLOUD CARS PASS LAZILY OUTSIDE THE WINDOW OF THE SUITE LANDO CALRISSIAN HAS PROVIDED THE FUGITIVE REBELS. FOR SOME TIME HAN SOLO HAS BEEN CONTENT TO IDLY WATCH THEM. UNTIL NOW, WHEN THE DOOR TO LEIA'S ROOM OPENS BEHIND HIM...
HAN, HAS THREEPIO TURNED UP YET...?
HUH...? OH YEAH... HE'S BEEN GONE TOO LONG TO BE JUST LOST.
BUT BEFORE WE ORGANIZE THE SEARCH PARTIES... LET ME GET A LOOK AT YOU! YOU LOOK GREAT!

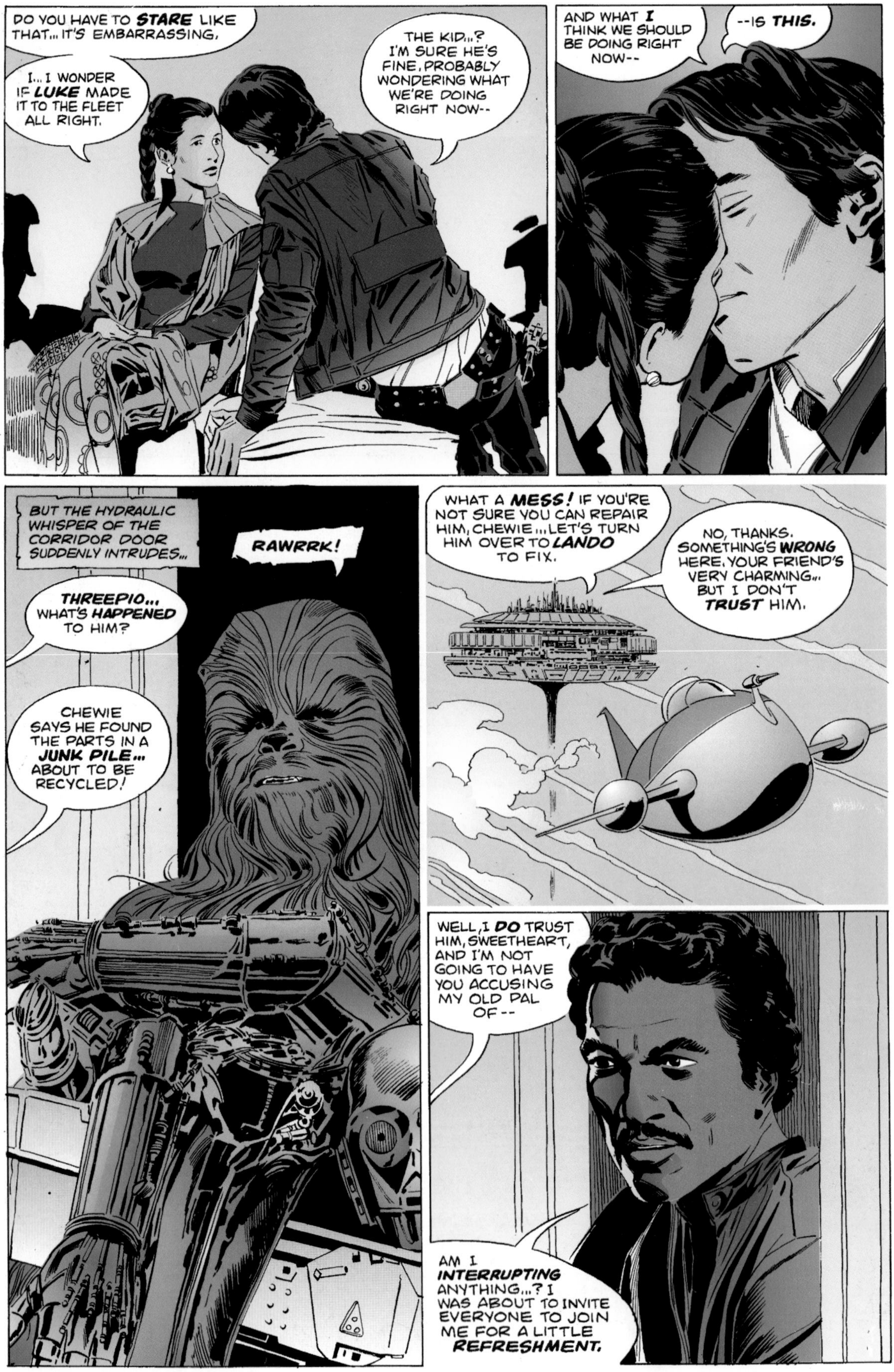
DO YOU HAVE TO STARE LIKE THAT... IT'S EMBARRASSING.
I... I WONDER IF LUKE MADE IT TO THE FLEET ALL RIGHT.
THE KID...? I'M SURE HE'S FINE, PROBABLY WONDERING WHAT WE'RE DOING RIGHT NOW--
AND WHAT I THINK WE SHOULD BE DOING RIGHT NOW--
--IS THIS.
BUT THE HYDRAULIC WHISPER OF THE CORRIDOR DOOR SUDDENLY INTRUDES...
RAWRRK!
THREEPIO... WHAT'S HAPPENED TO HIM?
CHEWIE SAYS HE FOUND THE PARTS IN A JUNK PILE... ABOUT TO BE RECYCLED!
WHAT A MESS! IF YOU'RE NOT SURE YOU CAN REPAIR HIM, CHEWIE... LET'S TURN HIM OVER TO LANDO TO FIX.
NO, THANKS. SOMETHING'S WRONG HERE. YOUR FRIEND'S VERY CHARMING... BUT I DON'T TRUST HIM.
WELL, I DO TRUST HIM, SWEETHEART, AND I'M NOT GOING TO HAVE YOU ACCUSING MY OLD PAL OF--
AM I INTERRUPTING ANYTHING...? I WAS ABOUT TO INVITE EVERYONE TO JOIN ME FOR A LITTLE REFRESHMENT.

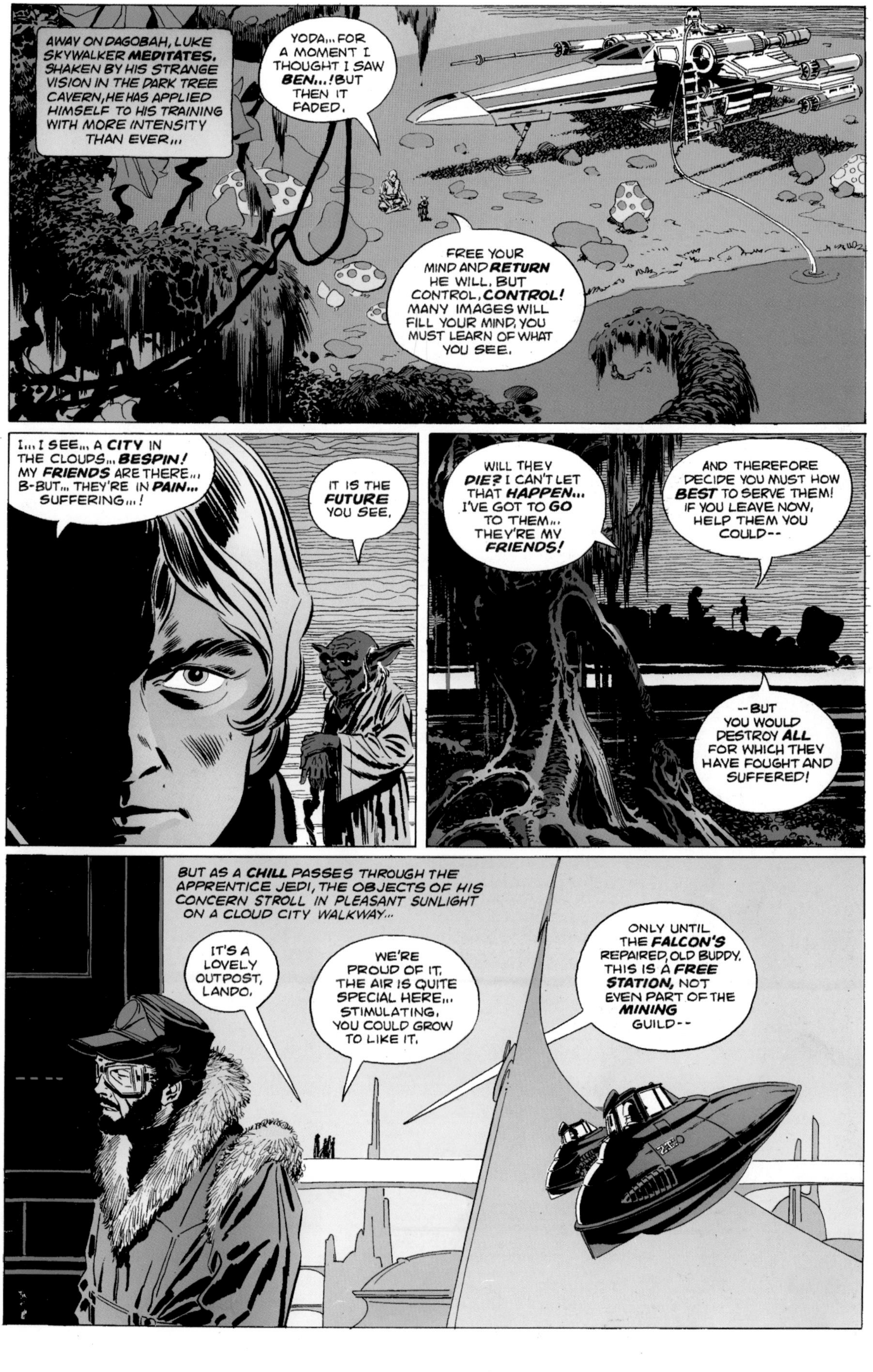

AWAY ON DAGOBAH, LUKE SKYWALKER **MEDITATES.** SHAKEN BY HIS STRANGE VISION IN THE DARK TREE CAVERN, HE HAS APPLIED HIMSELF TO HIS TRAINING WITH MORE INTENSITY THAN EVER...
YODA... FOR A MOMENT I THOUGHT I SAW **BEN...!** BUT THEN IT FADED.
FREE YOUR MIND AND **RETURN** HE WILL. BUT CONTROL, **CONTROL!** MANY IMAGES WILL FILL YOUR MIND, YOU MUST LEARN OF WHAT YOU SEE.
I... I SEE... A **CITY** IN THE CLOUDS... **BESPIN!** MY **FRIENDS** ARE THERE... B-BUT... THEY'RE IN **PAIN...** SUFFERING...!
IT IS THE **FUTURE** YOU SEE.
WILL THEY **DIE?** I CAN'T LET THAT **HAPPEN...** I'VE GOT TO **GO** TO THEM... THEY'RE MY **FRIENDS!**
AND THEREFORE DECIDE YOU MUST HOW **BEST** TO SERVE THEM! IF YOU LEAVE NOW, HELP THEM YOU COULD--
--BUT YOU WOULD DESTROY **ALL** FOR WHICH THEY HAVE FOUGHT AND SUFFERED!
BUT AS A **CHILL** PASSES THROUGH THE APPRENTICE JEDI, THE OBJECTS OF HIS CONCERN STROLL IN PLEASANT SUNLIGHT ON A CLOUD CITY WALKWAY...
IT'S A LOVELY OUTPOST, LANDO.
WE'RE PROUD OF IT. THE AIR IS QUITE SPECIAL HERE... STIMULATING. YOU COULD GROW TO LIKE IT.
ONLY UNTIL THE **FALCON'S** REPAIRED, OLD BUDDY. THIS IS A **FREE STATION,** NOT EVEN PART OF THE **MINING** GUILD--

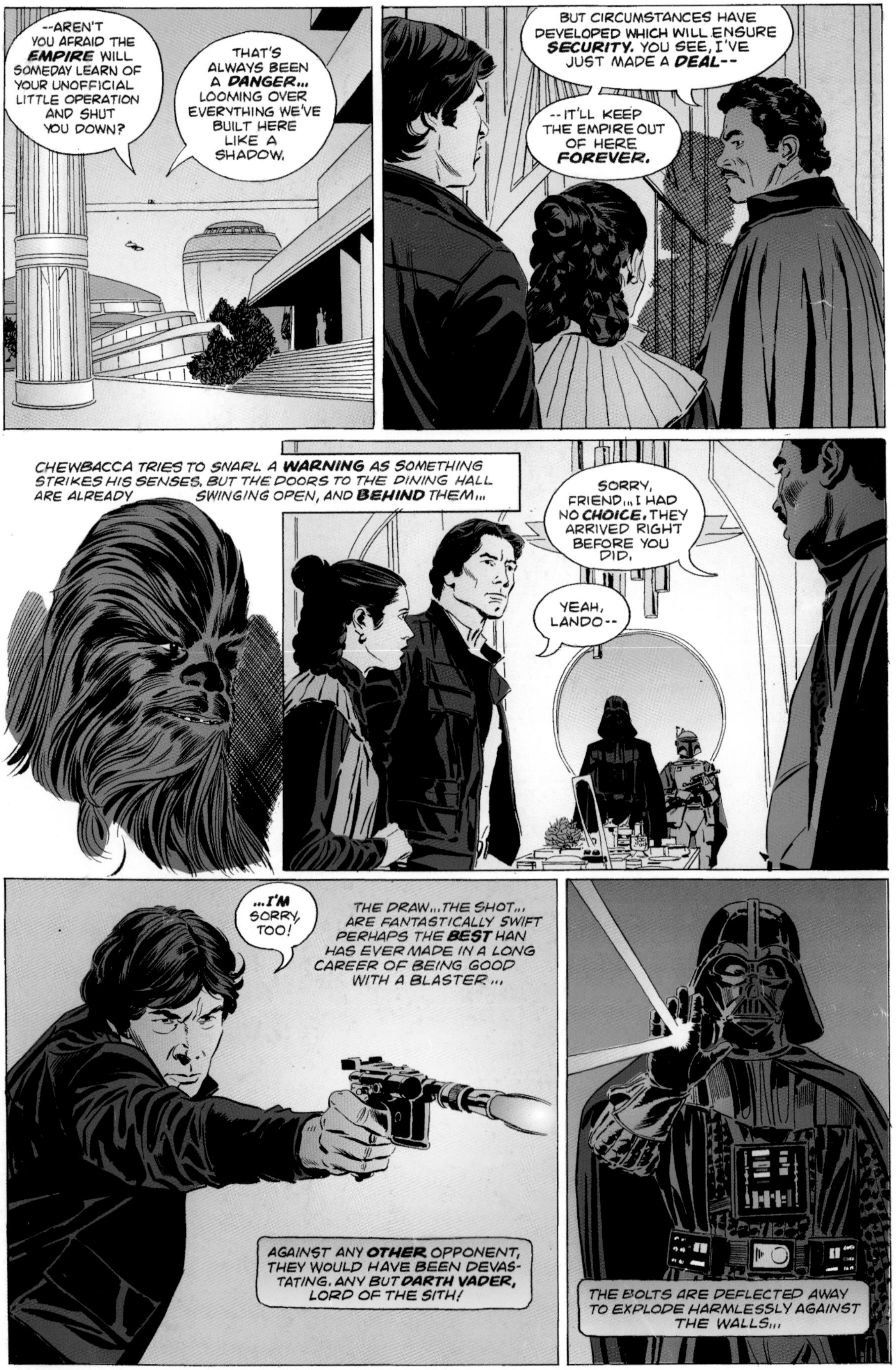

--AREN'T YOU AFRAID THE EMPIRE WILL SOMEDAY LEARN OF YOUR UNOFFICIAL LITTLE OPERATION AND SHUT YOU DOWN?
THAT'S ALWAYS BEEN A DANGER... LOOMING OVER EVERYTHING WE'VE BUILT HERE LIKE A SHADOW.
BUT CIRCUMSTANCES HAVE DEVELOPED WHICH WILL ENSURE SECURITY. YOU SEE, I'VE JUST MADE A DEAL--
--IT'LL KEEP THE EMPIRE OUT OF HERE FOREVER.
CHEWBACCA TRIES TO SNARL A WARNING AS SOMETHING STRIKES HIS SENSES, BUT THE DOORS TO THE DINING HALL ARE ALREADY SWINGING OPEN, AND BEHIND THEM...
SORRY, FRIEND... I HAD NO CHOICE. THEY ARRIVED RIGHT BEFORE YOU DID.
YEAH, LANDO--
...I'M SORRY, TOO!
THE DRAW... THE SHOT... ARE FANTASTICALLY SWIFT PERHAPS THE BEST HAN HAS EVER MADE IN A LONG CAREER OF BEING GOOD WITH A BLASTER...
AGAINST ANY OTHER OPPONENT, THEY WOULD HAVE BEEN DEVAS-TATING. ANY BUT DARTH VADER, LORD OF THE SITH!
THE BOLTS ARE DEFLECTED AWAY TO EXPLODE HARMLESSLY AGAINST THE WALLS...